THE SKYWALKER SAGA

WRITTEN BY DELILAH S. DAWSON
ILLUSTRATED BY BRIAN ROOD

PRESS
Los Angeles • New York

For information address Disney • Lucasfilm Press,
1200 Grand Central Avenue, Glendale, California 91201.

Printed in the United States of America

First Edition, October 2019

1 3 5 7 9 10 8 6 4 2

Library of Congress Control Number on file

FAC-038091-19235

ISBN 978-1-368-04153-9

Visit the official *Star Wars* website at: www.starwars.com.

CONTENTS

A long time ago in a galaxy far,
far away. . . .

THE PHANTOM MENACE

Once upon a time, in a galaxy far, far away, there was a desert planet by the name of Tatooine. It was a dry, lonely place where long-necked rontos, leathery dewbacks, and furry banthas roamed the hot sand under twin suns. Aliens and star pilots gathered to trade goods or watch podraces in small settlements while Jawas trundled across the dunes in their lumbering sandcrawlers, scavenging for droid parts. Tatooine was a quiet planet, largely ignored by the rest of the galaxy, and most beings there didn't dare dream of a greater life.

Meanwhile, on the bustling central world of Coruscant, the Galactic Senate thoughtfully governed thousands of planets while the Jedi Knights of the noble Jedi Order acted as guardians of peace and justice. But when the greedy Trade Federation chose to defy the Galactic Senate and blockade the idyllic planet of Naboo with its battleships, two Jedi Knights were sent to intervene.

However, the Jedi's attempted negotiations were short-lived, and they were forced to make a daring escape, ultimately fleeing to Tatooine to repair their ship so they could return to the Galactic Senate and report on the Trade Federation's actions.

Little did the Jedi know that landing on the small, sandy planet would change the fate of the galaxy forever. . . .

Anakin Skywalker had lived on Tatooine all his life.

He was just a young boy, so it hadn't been a very long life, but it had *felt* long. Anakin was a slave, and he worked in a junk shop with his mother, Shmi.

But one day something unusual happened: three strangers showed up with an astromech droid. They needed parts for their ship, and Anakin's master, Watto — a flying blue alien with a long wrinkly nose — was always eager to make a deal. As the strange man from the party, Qui-Gon Jinn, went to bargain with Watto, Anakin was left to watch the shop — and meet the other outlanders: a floppy-eared Gungan named Jar Jar Binks and a young woman named Padmé.

"Are you an angel?" Anakin asked Padmé, catching her by surprise. "I heard the deep-space pilots talk about them. They're the most beautiful creatures in the universe."

Padmé smiled mischievously, but Anakin

noticed she didn't deny being an angel.

"You're a funny little boy. How do you know so much?"

Anakin's temper flared, that she would think of him as little. She couldn't be that much older than him! He was nine, and he figured she was about fourteen.

"I listen to all the traders and pilots who come through here. I'm a pilot," he told her proudly, "and someday I'm going to fly away from this place."

Anakin dreamed of freedom and adventure, and he had seen a lightsaber – the laser weapon of the Jedi Knights – hidden under Qui-Gon's robe.

So when the man was unable to forge a deal with Watto, Anakin invited the strangers to take shelter in his home from a dangerous sandstorm that was approaching.

The young boy was sure the outlanders had come into his life for a reason, and he wasn't eager to see them go.

Anakin introduced his new friends to his mother and showed Padmé a protocol droid he was building named C-3PO. Padmé was impressed and called C-3PO perfect, but her astromech droid, R2-D2, laughed at the unfinished droid, using his language of beeps to call him naked.

"My parts are showing?" the confused protocol droid asked. "Oh, my goodness!"

Over dinner, Anakin watched Qui-Gon Jinn, finally asking, "You're a Jedi Knight, aren't you?"

"What makes you think that?" Qui-Gon replied.

"I saw your laser sword. Only Jedis carry that kind of weapon."

Qui-Gon looked amused. "Perhaps I killed a Jedi and took it from him."

Anakin shook his head. "I don't think so. No one can kill a Jedi."

At that, Qui-Gon looked sad. "I wish that were so."

Then Anakin told Qui-Gon a secret he had never told anyone before.

"I had a dream I was a Jedi. I came back here and freed all the slaves. Have you come to free us?"

The older man couldn't quite meet Anakin's eyes. "No, I'm afraid not."

But Anakin didn't believe him. "I think you have. Why else would you be here?"

Qui-Gon paused a moment, as if he'd made a decision. "I can see there's no fooling you, Anakin. We're on our way to Coruscant on a very important mission."

He and Padmé explained the conflict between the honorable Galactic Senate and the greedy Trade Federation. The leader of the Trade Federation, Viceroy Gunray, had held Naboo's queen, Amidala, captive in her palace, but

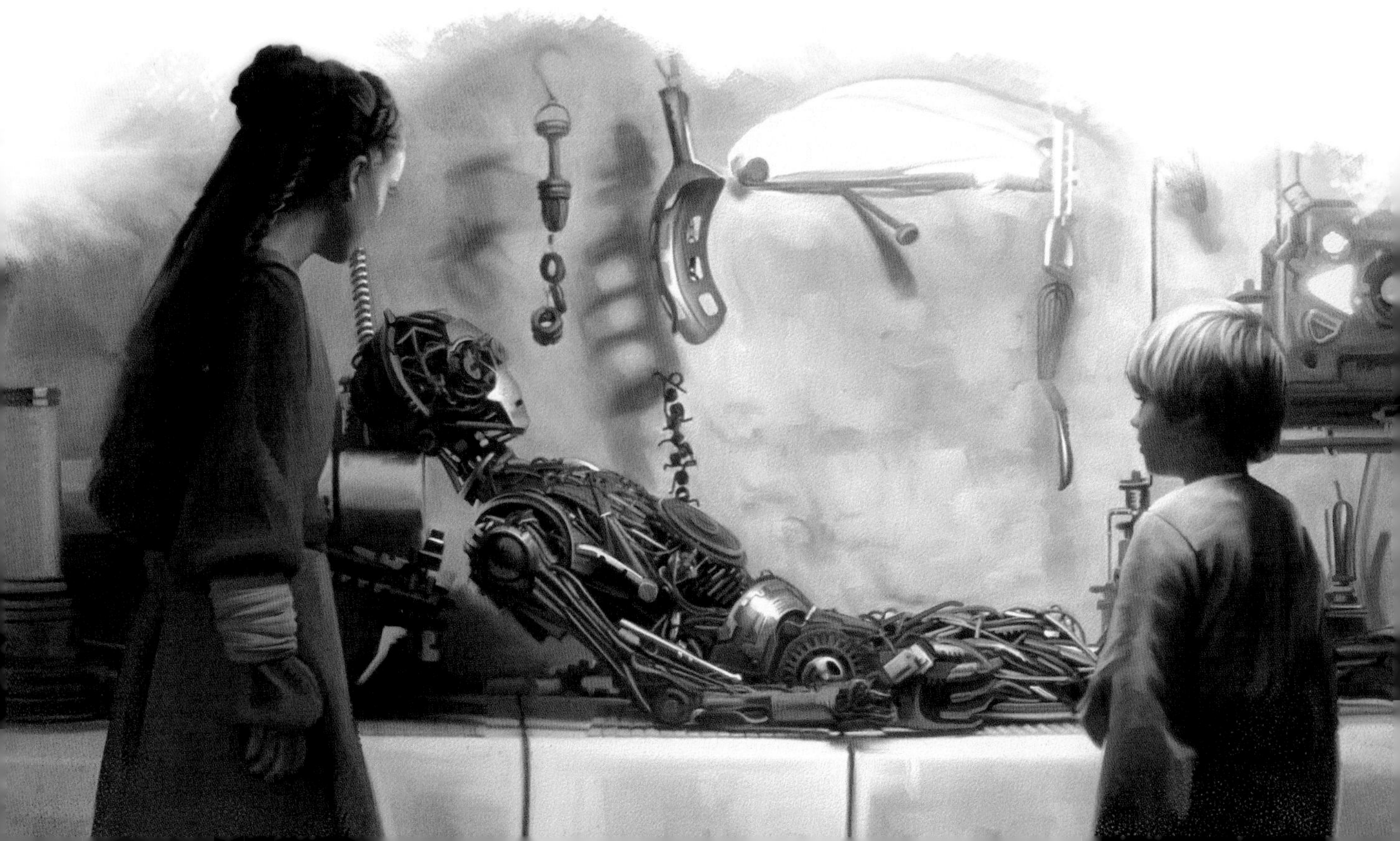

Qui-Gon and his apprentice, Obi-Wan Kenobi, had rescued the queen and escaped from Naboo. Padmé was one of the queen's handmaidens, and Jar Jar was a fellow citizen of Naboo. They were all stranded on Tatooine until they could repair Queen Amidala's ship. Watto had the parts they needed, but they had no money to pay him.

However, Anakin knew there was one thing the cunning junk dealer couldn't resist: a bet. Their whole settlement of Mos Espa ran on gambling, especially when it came to podracing.

"I've built a racer!" Anakin told them. "It's the fastest ever. There's a big race tomorrow for Boonta Eve. You could enter my pod. The prize money would more than pay for the parts you need."

"I don't want you to race, Ani," Shmi said with a shiver. "It's awful."

Anakin hated to make his mother worry, but he knew that someone had to do the right thing.

"We have to help them, Mom. You said the biggest problem in this universe is that nobody helps each other."

How could he make her see how important this was, how much he felt like it was up to him to help?

"I'm sure Qui-Gon doesn't want to put your son in danger," Padmé said gently. "We will find another way."

"No, Ani's right." His mother looked down as if the words hurt to say. "There is no other way. He was meant to help you."

Anakin was thrilled. His mother shared a strange look with Qui-Gon. But Qui-Gon did not say no.

"Is that a yes?" Anakin asked, needing to hear the words spoken, needing it to be real. "That's a yes!"

The next day, Anakin arrived in Watto's workshop with a sense of hope he'd never felt before. After much discussion, Qui-Gon and Watto reached an agreement: if Anakin won the race, Qui-Gon could have the parts he needed to fix the queen's ship and Watto would keep the winnings. However, if Anakin lost — which he was sure he wouldn't — Qui-Gon had to give the queen's ship to Watto, leaving Qui-Gon with nothing and stranding his entire party and Queen Amidala on Tatooine.

It was a wonderful feeling for Anakin, knowing the Jedi had faith in him. But it was also intimidating, knowing that the fate of so many rested on his small shoulders.

That night, as Qui-Gon helped Anakin clean up a cut, the boy felt something prick his arm. Qui-Gon had used a small device to collect some of Anakin's blood.

When Anakin asked him what he was doing, the Jedi said he was just checking Anakin's blood for infections.

The boy was fairly certain that Qui-Gon was lying, but before he could probe any further, his mother called him to bed. He lay awake for hours thinking about the next day's race.

What Anakin didn't realize was that when Qui-Gon had his blood analyzed, the Jedi discovered that the young slave boy from Tatooine had higher Jedi markers than any Jedi in history.

The following morning, Anakin stood on the track beside his podracer, which looked shabby next to all the other racers' souped-up machines. Each ship had a cockpit for the pilot, which was pulled along by two big engines. Most humans couldn't think and navigate quickly enough to race, but Anakin seemed to have special abilities.

The stands were full of excited spectators, all waving flags or watching the race on specialized screens. People from all over the galaxy were there, including the most powerful gangster of all and the race's host, the sluglike Jabba the Hutt. But Anakin didn't let the pageantry distract him. He readied his podracer and prepared his mind for the most important race of his life.

Jar Jar wished him well and left to join Shmi in the stands. Padmé kissed him on the cheek, and then only Qui-Gon was left.

"Remember: Concentrate on the moment. Feel, don't think. Trust your instincts." As he spoke, the Jedi gave Anakin a significant look, and the boy felt as if the older man was no longer talking about the race.

"May the Force be with you," Qui-Gon concluded, referring to the mystical energy field created by all living things that gave the Jedi their power and bound the galaxy together.

Anakin was left to himself, turning the phrase over in his mind.

High up in the stands, Jabba spat a gorg head against a gong, and the race began!

Or . . . it should have.

When Anakin fired up his engines, his podracer stalled out. The other racers took off. Thousands of people in the stands began to laugh at him, and the two-headed Troig announcer bellowed, "He'll be hard-pressed to catch up with the leaders now!"

Still, Anakin centered himself, remained calm, and hunted for the problem.

There! The fuel regulator was open, which had caused the engines to flood. How had that happened?

Sebulba, Anakin thought. The dangerous and competitive Dug podracer hated to lose.

At last his engines ignited and Anakin took off. Already, a podracer had exploded against the rocks, and Anakin knew many more perils awaited him. Sebulba was always sabotaging the other podracers, and Anakin passed several flaming crashes and watched other podracers malfunction or explode. Screeching Tusken Raiders aimed their guns from the desert cliffs, their shots pinging off Anakin's hull. But the boy only moved closer to the front of the pack.

In the last lap, Anakin finally caught up to Sebulba, who rammed Anakin's podracer with his own, forcing the boy onto a service ramp. But the gambit backfired as Anakin used his height to drop directly in front of the vicious Dug's podracer. Sebulba didn't like that and tried every trick in the book – tricks Anakin knew well and countered – right up until the final straightaway, when Sebulba shoved him again, hard, and their podracers became entangled.

Anakin remembered what Qui-Gon had said. He quieted his mind, focusing on the task at hand, and with a sudden thrust pulled his podracer away from Sebulba's and zoomed across the finish line as the Dug's podracer flailed to a halt!

Anakin had won the race!

Qui-Gon lifted the boy high as Shmi, Padmé, and Jar Jar ran up to congratulate him.

"Mom, I did it!" Anakin said, beaming.

"We owe you everything," Padmé said.

With the parts they needed to repair their ship, the Jedi would soon be leaving. But Qui-Gon returned to Anakin's home once more. He had sold the boy's podracer, and he gave the credits to Anakin, who proudly handed them to his mother. Then Qui-Gon told Anakin something the young boy never thought he would hear. . . .

"You're no longer a slave."

Anakin was shocked. Qui-Gon had worked out a deal with Watto for Anakin's freedom.

"Now you can make your dreams come true, Ani," his mother said before turning to Qui-Gon. "Will you take him with you? Is he to become a Jedi?"

"Yes," Qui-Gon said. "Our meeting was not a coincidence. Nothing happens by accident."

Anakin's heart skipped a beat. This was his dream, his secret desire: to become a Jedi Knight and travel the galaxy helping those in need.

But then a heavy thought entered his mind. "What about Mom?"

The Jedi looked solemn. "I tried to free your mother, Ani. But Watto wouldn't have it."

Anakin couldn't believe it. His mother had worked so hard to protect him. Could he really just leave her?

The boy looked down, feeling tears prick his eyes. All slaves were fitted with an explosive chip, and if Shmi left the planet without being freed, she would meet a swift and ugly end. She couldn't go with them, not if Watto wouldn't release her.

Anakin's mother pulled him close.

"Son, my place is here. My future is here. It is time for you to let go."

"I don't want things to change," Anakin told her.

With soft and steady wisdom, Shmi replied, "You can't stop change, any more than you can stop the suns from setting." She hugged him tightly before turning him around to face Qui-Gon. "Now hurry!" she told him, and he ran into his room to pack his bag and say good-bye to C-3PO.

But as Anakin left home, following Qui-Gon, he stopped to look back once more. When he saw the tears in his mother's eyes, all his fears swelled up inside him. He ran back to her, and Shmi dropped to her knees to hug him.

"I can't do it, Mom. Will I ever see you again?"

"What does your heart tell you?"

He wasn't sure. "I hope so. Yes. I guess."

She smiled. "Then we *will* see each other again."

"I will come back and free you, Mom. I promise."

Shmi stood. "Now, be brave, and don't look back."

She gave her son a gentle push, and Anakin did exactly what she said. He followed Qui-Gon and didn't look back.

It wasn't a long journey back to the ship, but as Qui-Gon and Anakin approached the shiny cruiser, Anakin realized he had never felt so weary.

"Qui-Gon, sir! Wait! I'm tired!" he called.

But when Qui-Gon turned around, his gaze swept past Anakin, and his eyes grew wide.

"Anakin, drop!"

Hearing the alarm in the Jedi's voice and feeling his own cold trill of disquiet, Anakin dove to the sand and felt the air ruffle his hair as a speeder bike zipped overhead—mere centimeters away. He looked up in time to see a black-robed figure do a flip off the speeder and land with a lightsaber in hand, igniting the red blade just as Qui-Gon ignited his own weapon.

The fight began as Anakin rose to his feet, and Qui-Gon shouted, "Go! Tell them to take off!"

It was riveting, the two men sparring with real lightsabers, but Anakin knew he had his own role to play. He ran toward the ship, the red and green blades zapping and buzzing as they clashed behind him. When he made it up the ramp, he told Padmé what Qui-Gon had said. In the cockpit, a younger Jedi ordered the pilot to take off, directing him to fly low. The ship lifted into the air and lowered its ramp, and Qui-Gon disengaged from the warrior to bound onto the ship, barely escaping his vicious foe.

"What was it?" the younger Jedi asked Qui-Gon.

"I'm not sure, but it was well trained in the Jedi arts. My guess is it was after the queen."

"What are we going to do about it?" Anakin asked.

"We shall be patient," Qui-Gon said as he held out a hand. "Anakin Skywalker, meet Obi-Wan Kenobi."

Anakin shook the younger Jedi's hand as the ship blasted away from Tatooine and into the galaxy he'd always longed to see for himself.

Life away from Watto's shop was already proving to be exciting — and dangerous.

Anakin shivered on a bench inside the ship. It was a long journey to Coruscant, and he'd been cold since the moment they'd left Tatooine's atmosphere. Anakin wasn't used to the black chill of space.

He saw Padmé watching a holomessage from an official back on Naboo. The man in the message spoke urgently, with terror in his flickering blue eyes. When Padmé noticed Anakin watching her from the corner, she found a blanket and tucked it around the boy.

"You seem sad," said Anakin.

"The queen is worried," Padmé replied. "Her people are suffering — dying. She must convince the Senate to intervene, or . . . I'm not sure what will happen."

Anakin pulled a simple necklace with a hand-carved token from beneath the blanket.

"I made this for you, so you'd remember me. I carved it," the boy said. "It will bring you good fortune."

Padmé was touched by Anakin's gift.

"It's beautiful, but I don't need this to remember you by," she said with a smile. "Many things will change when we reach the capital, Ani, but my caring for you will remain."

Anakin was comforted by Padmé's words. Even though he had left Tatooine, Padmé's presence felt like a piece of home. She was kind, and he knew he could trust her.

When Coruscant came into view, Anakin was stunned to see that the planet was covered by one giant city. The ship landed on a platform among the clouds, where the queen's party was met by Senator Palpatine and Supreme Chancellor Valorum, two stern, gray-haired men from the Galactic Senate. Anakin was whisked away with Padmé and Jar Jar in an air taxi to an ornate apartment that overlooked the bustling city while Qui-Gon and Obi-Wan reported back to the Jedi Temple.

Later in the day, it was Anakin's turn to meet the Jedi, but he wanted to say good-bye to Padmé first. He knew that if he became a student of the Jedi, he might never see his friend again. When he went to find her, he found Queen Amidala instead.

The queen looked weary, as if her large headdress, red robes, and ornate makeup weighed heavily on her. Anakin had overheard Senator Palpatine urging her to elect a new supreme chancellor for the Senate, someone who might be more sympathetic to Naboo's plight than the current leader, Supreme Chancellor Valorum. Anakin could tell that Queen Amidala was torn about the decision.

She told him that she had sent Padmé on an errand.

"We are sure her heart goes with you," the queen assured him, but Anakin's own heart seemed to sink inside his chest. He missed his mother, and now he would miss Padmé, too.

Anakin was taken before the Jedi High Council, a circle of twelve Jedi Masters gathered in a tower atop the Jedi Temple. The tests the Jedi Masters gave him were rigorous, and Anakin could feel the powerful beings' consideration like a palpable force. When Mace Windu, an intense human man with a penetrating gaze, asked him to name the objects appearing on a screen he couldn't see, Anakin felt the knowledge rise up as if he'd plucked the information directly from the serious Jedi's mind.

Yoda, a small green alien with a bald, wrinkled head and big ears, eyed the boy.

"How feel you?" Yoda asked, his three-fingered hand resting on his small chin.

"Cold, sir," Anakin answered. Even as the sun set, bathing the room in flaming shades of red and orange, Anakin felt as if he would never know warmth again.

"Afraid, are you?"

"No, sir."

But Yoda knew better.

"See through you, we can," he said.

Anakin struggled to stay outwardly calm. He tried to ignore his fear, but of course the Jedi would sense it.

Mace leaned forward. "Be mindful of your feelings."

"Your thoughts dwell on your mother," added Ki-Adi-Mundi, a tall Cerean Jedi Master with a cone-shaped head.

"I miss her," Anakin admitted.

Yoda nodded. "Afraid to lose her, I think, hmmm?"

"What has that got to do with anything?" Anakin asked. He had shown the Jedi his skills, and he knew they'd been impressed. What did his feelings about his old life have to do with his future as a Jedi?

"Everything!" Yoda said. "Fear is the path to the dark side. Fear leads to anger. Anger leads to hate. Hate leads to suffering."

Anakin tried to understand Yoda's words, but they confused him. He'd only just landed on that new planet; how could he forget his mother so soon? As the Jedi Council considered him, he forced himself to stand tall.

"I sense much fear in you," Yoda finally said, almost apologetically.

Then the Jedi excused Anakin so they could deliberate over his fate.

Later that night, Anakin stood again in the Jedi Council Chamber, but he was flanked by Qui-Gon and Obi-Wan.

"The Force is strong with him," Ki-Adi-Mundi began in a kindly voice.

"He is to be trained, then?" Qui-Gon asked.

Mace Windu's face was as hard as stone. "No, he will not be trained."

Qui-Gon was surprised. "No?"

"He is too old."

"He is the *chosen one*. You must see it," Qui-Gon argued, referring to an old Jedi prophecy that spoke of one who would bring balance to the Force.

"Mmm. Clouded, this boy's future is," Yoda mused.

Anakin could feel Qui-Gon's frustration, but what he said next was unexpected. "I will train him, then." The Jedi's hands settled heavily on Anakin's shoulders. "I take Anakin as my Padawan learner."

"An apprentice, you have, Qui-Gon," Yoda chided, nodding in Obi-Wan's direction. "Impossible to take on a second."

"The code forbids it," Mace added.

"Young Skywalker's fate will be decided later," Yoda said with finality.

Mace went on to explain that the Senate had voted for a new chancellor. Senator Palpatine would be the new leader of the Senate, and Queen Amidala was returning home to Naboo, which meant the confrontation with the Trade Federation would only grow worse. The Jedi were also concerned that the mysterious black-robed warrior who had attacked Qui-Gon might return. Qui-Gon was charged with the task of accompanying the queen to Naboo, with the hopes of also discovering more about the attacker.

Anakin bowed with Qui-Gon and Obi-Wan and left the room, still uncertain of his destiny among the Jedi.

It wasn't long before Anakin sat on a platform with R2, waiting to depart for Naboo. He couldn't help overhearing as Obi-Wan spoke to Qui-Gon with frustration.

"The boy is dangerous. They all sense it. Why can't you?"

Qui-Gon, at least, recognized that Anakin was listening. "His fate is uncertain. He's not dangerous. The Council will decide Anakin's future."

When Anakin told Qui-Gon he didn't want to be a problem, the Jedi reassured him. "You won't be, Ani. I'm not allowed to train you, so I want you to watch me and be mindful. Always remember: Your focus determines your reality. Stay close to me, and you'll be safe."

Even though his destiny was hazy, Anakin was free, and he would soon see a new planet. The queen's ship blasted into space and arrived in the Naboo system. After avoiding a Droid Control Ship, they landed in a rich green forest. Anakin had never seen any place so . . . alive. Trees, grass, vines, and wildlife made a riot of color and sound as their party waited beside a swamp for Jar Jar to contact his people. The Gungan returned from his visit to the underwater city to report that it was empty. Fortunately, Jar Jar knew the sacred place where the Gungans hid to avoid trouble.

They found the Gungans in the forest around an ancient temple. The large, froglike leader, Boss Nass, was not pleased to see Jar Jar Binks, who had been banished for past misadventures. But as the queen requested an alliance, something happened that took Anakin completely by surprise: Padmé the handmaiden stepped forward and announced that *she* was actually Queen Amidala! By revealing her decoy, she demonstrated trust in Boss Nass and showed him great deference.

"I ask you to help us," she said. Then, kneeling, she added, "I beg you to help us."

For a tense moment, Anakin wasn't sure if the Gungans would agree, but eventually, Boss Nass laughed. He had always assumed the humans of Naboo were proud and arrogant, and the queen's humility pleased him.

"Meesa like dis!" he chortled.

Soon the Gungans and humans were working together to plan their next move.

Amidala's loyal guard, Captain Panaka, told the queen that she could not beat the Trade Federation's droid army, which was controlled by an orbiting command ship that was also the source of the blockade. But Amidala revealed that the battle was just a diversion to draw the droid army away from the cities.

During the fight, Amidala and her forces would sneak into the palace to capture the Trade Federation's leader. Without Viceroy Gunray, the Trade Federation would be lost and confused. As part of the plan, Amidala would send her pilots to disable the Droid Control Ship floating near Naboo, which would render the droid army useless.

There were many ways the plan could fail, but Amidala had great confidence in her team.

Enacting the first part of the plan, the Gungans sent their soldiers into battle. Jar Jar and his fellow Gungans marched, rode tall animals called kaadus, tugged wagons of booma energy balls behind large beasts called falumpasets, and carried energy shields on the backs of their biggest four-legged beasts of burden, fambaas.

The Gungans activated giant shield generators that protected their soldiers under massive domes of energy. The blasts and bombs of the droid army fizzled harmlessly against the purple-tinted shields.

It was an impressive show of force, and Anakin wished he could watch them in battle. Instead, he went with Amidala and the Jedi to infiltrate the palace and take the viceroy captive.

It was strange for Anakin to know that his friend Padmé had always been Queen Amidala, and stranger still for him to see her carrying a blaster, which Captain Panaka assured Anakin the queen could use with great skill.

Qui-Gon, however, was concerned about *Anakin's* safety.

"Once we get inside, find a safe place to hide and stay there."

After they'd blasted their way into the palace's hangar, Amidala ordered her pilots to get to their ships. Anakin ran here and there, trying to find somewhere safe. But no matter where he went, blaster bolts followed him.

Amidala's pilots leapt into the ships, their astromech droids already in place, and zoomed out of the hangar into the blue sky, then on to the blackness of space.

When R2 was suddenly pulled up into a starship, Anakin realized that ships, at least, had shields, so he scrambled into the cockpit. Once all the ships were out of the hangar, Amidala ordered her people to head for the throne room, where the viceroy would be hiding.

"Hey, wait for me!" Anakin called.

"Stay where you are," Qui-Gon ordered him. "You'll be safe there."

But as the door to the palace opened, a terrifying figure was revealed: the mysterious black-robed warrior!

"We'll handle this," Qui-Gon said, striding forward with Obi-Wan.

The two Jedi shook off their outer cloaks and ignited their lightsabers as the dark warrior pulled back his own hood to reveal the red skin, tattooed face, and head horns of a Zabrak. His red eyes glowed as bright as the double-bladed lightsaber he ignited.

Amidala and her guards hurried off to continue their mission, but three deadly droidekas rolled into view, deployed their shields, and started firing!

Anakin watched as Amidala's contingent was pinned down, unable to penetrate the droids' shields.

"We've got to do something, Artoo!" he said.

Trying to shoot the droids, Anakin accidentally powered up his ship and triggered its autopilot function. As the ship rolled toward the hangar door, he found the gun's controls and eliminated all three droidekas, allowing Amidala to escape.

But then Anakin was in space in a strange starship, its automatic pilot drawing him helplessly toward the battle surrounding one of the droid control ships.

Anakin's fellow Naboo starfighter pilots took on enemy fire all around him as he fought to take control of his own ship. He sensed that if he could fly the ship himself, he could make a difference in the battle. R2 got to work, disengaging the autopilot function, and soon Anakin's natural flying skills took over.

He found that Qui-Gon's instructions before the podrace still applied: *Concentrate on the moment. Feel, don't think. Trust your instincts.* When he listened to his instincts, it was as though the ship responded to his every whim.

But, suddenly, Anakin's ship took a hit and he lost control. Anakin barely managed to avoid a catastrophic crash as he steered the starfighter into the hangar of the huge Droid Control Ship.

Anakin's ship slid to a screeching halt on the floor of the enemy hangar. Armed droids ran from every direction, and Anakin began pushing buttons, hoping for a miracle.

For one long, dark moment, as the droids ran toward him, Anakin felt as though all was lost. Far below him on Naboo, his friends were faring no better.

Amidala and her guards had been captured by the Trade Federation's viceroy, as opposed to the other way around. And out on the battlefield, the Gungans were in for a nasty surprise.

When the droids' cannons had no effect on the Gungans' protective shields, the droid army deployed thousands of individual battle droids instead. The droids unfurled from their

containment ships, simultaneously reaching for their blasters, and marched ominously toward the Gungan forces.

Jar Jar looked nervously at the encroaching mechanical soldiers.

A fellow Gungan gulped. "Ouch time."

Somehow, the droids were able to simply *walk* through the protective shields completely unharmed! Chaos erupted underneath the domes of energy as the Gungans scrambled to fight back against the barrage of blasts from the droid soldiers and rolling droidekas.

But try as the Gungans might, it was no use. The droid army was relentless. It wasn't long before the valiant Gungan army had surrendered to the droid soldiers entirely.

Meanwhile, the fight between Qui-Gon, Obi-Wan, and the black-clad menace had spilled out of the hangar and into a generator complex. The three warriors battled along dangerous catwalks and down long hallways segmented by force fields that would suddenly flicker on and off, making it impossible to pass through.

The Jedi Knights fiercely dueled the Zabrak warrior, lightsabers clashing against lightsabers while the three men called on the Force to leap and flip over and away from one another as though they were engaged in some sort of dangerous dance.

At one point, Obi-Wan became separated from Qui-Gon and the dark warrior, and was kept back from the battle by a thrumming force field. Obi-Wan had no choice but to watch helplessly as his master continued the fight on his own. Qui-Gon Jinn was strong, but the Zabrak seemed stronger, full of anger that fueled his dark power.

Suddenly, a force field appeared between Qui-Gon and the red-faced warrior. Qui-Gon took that moment to kneel, quieting his mind and calling on the Force while his opponent paced back and forth, eager to finish the battle.

When the force field between the two fizzled

away, Obi-Wan watched in horror as Qui-Gon sprang into action, only to be stopped forever by a swift slash of the dark warrior's red saber.

As soon as the force field in front of him disappeared, Obi-Wan ran forward, desperate to right the terrible wrong that had just occurred. He called on every ounce of his training and let himself be guided by the light side of the Force as he sparred and parried with the dark foe. He even managed to slice part of the warrior's lightsaber hilt, reducing his enemy's double-sided weapon to just one red energy blade.

In a crucial moment, the Zabrak was able to summon the dark side of the Force to push Obi-Wan over the edge of the reactor shaft. The Jedi lost his lightsaber, but he managed to grab hold of a fixture and stop his fall.

Obi-Wan sensed Qui-Gon's lightsaber nearby. Calling on the Force, the Jedi leapt from the reactor shaft, summoning Qui-Gon's blade and igniting it as he flipped up and over the Zabrak, dealing a deadly blow. The warrior stumbled, falling back toward the reactor shaft and plummeting to unknown depths. Obi-Wan Kenobi had triumphed, but his victory was bittersweet. His master was gone.

In the Droid Control Ship far overhead, R2 beeped and Anakin's ship powered back to life. Blaster fire pinged off his shields, and Anakin returned fire.The boy let his instincts take over, and a lucky shot hit the main reactor!

Thanks to Anakin, a series of explosions rocked the Droid Control Ship, cutting off all power, and the boy zoomed out of the main hold as the Trade Federation's command ship exploded in a shower of sparks!

Down on Naboo, the droid soldiers froze in place. Without the command ship, the once dangerous robots were no longer a threat. The Gungans celebrated with raucous cheers.

And once again using her decoy queen as a diversion, Amidala captured the evil Viceroy Gunray.

Amidala's plan had succeeded. The Trade Federation's reign of terror was finally over.

A ship arrived to take the Trade Federation viceroy to Coruscant to answer for his crimes. It also brought the new supreme chancellor of the Galactic Senate, Naboo's own Senator Palpatine, who commended Obi-Wan for his service and singled out Anakin for praise.

"We will watch your career with great interest, Young Skywalker," the older man said, patting Anakin on the arm and making him feel just as important as the older Jedi.

But the excitement did not last, for Anakin learned that Qui-Gon Jinn had been killed by the mysterious warrior. The boy stood with Obi-Wan at Qui-Gon's funeral, and Anakin felt more lost than ever.

"What will happen to me now?" he asked.

"The Council have granted me permission to train you. You will be a Jedi, I promise," Obi-Wan told him.

But as Anakin gazed at the funeral pyre, he realized that being a Jedi was a hard life, and often, Anakin was learning, it ended all too soon.

Nearby, Yoda and Mace Windu spoke quietly.

"There's no doubt the mysterious warrior was a Sith," Mace said, referring to the dark sect of Force-sensitive individuals who used their powers for evil.

Yoda nodded, thoughtful. "Always two there are. No more, no less. A master and an apprentice."

"But which was destroyed? The master or the apprentice?" Mace replied.

They knew that somewhere in the galaxy, there was still a threat.

But that was a worry for another time. There was much to celebrate first, and a grand parade was held to honor Naboo's victory.

Gungans in bright uniforms marched through the city streets, playing drums and horns. Ships zoomed overhead in formation, and the crowd waved colorful pennants as confetti rained from the sky.

Wearing his first Jedi robes, Anakin stood between R2 and Obi-Wan, along with Supreme Chancellor Palpatine, Captain Panaka, and Queen Amidala, who wore a pale pink gown and looked like the angel Anakin had once mistaken her for.

Amidala stepped forward to present Boss Nass and Jar Jar with the Globe of Peace to symbolize ongoing cooperation between the humans and Gungans of Naboo.

When Amidala turned to look at Anakin, he swelled with pride and returned her smile.

Anakin would become a Jedi, and like his new friend Queen Amidala, he would help spread peace throughout the galaxy.

ATTACK OF THE CLONES

In the far reaches of space, a young boy named Anakin Skywalker learned the ancient ways of the Jedi, an order of knights who protected the galaxy from harm. Soon the boy had grown into a young man and a talented warrior under the tutelage of Jedi Knight Obi-Wan Kenobi.

But the galaxy was fraught with unrest. An evil faction known as the Separatists—led by a former Jedi, Count Dooku—worked to overthrow the galaxy's governing body, the Galactic Republic.

The Separatists had even threatened the life of the young senator and former queen Padmé Amidala.

The head of the Senate, Chancellor Palpatine, asked Obi-Wan Kenobi and Anakin Skywalker to shadow the senator and protect her from all possible threats, be they seen or unseen. . . .

Anakin Skywalker was more excited than he'd ever been in his life. He had been waiting for this day for such a long time.

He stood beside Obi-Wan Kenobi in a lift carrying them up into a tower on Coruscant. Outside, sunshine bathed the buildings and spires in rose-gold light and flashed off speeders and spaceships, but Anakin could only stare at the door and fiddle anxiously with his brown Jedi robes.

"You seem a little on edge," Obi-Wan observed, looking every bit the wise, calm Jedi Master.

Anakin exhaled. Of course he couldn't fool Obi-Wan. "I haven't seen her in ten years," he finally admitted. Obi-Wan just smiled.

The lift door opened, and the Jedi were led to meet Senator Padmé Amidala, the young woman Anakin had known as a friend long before, when he was just a boy.

"Ani? My goodness, you've grown."

Padmé was as beautiful as Anakin remembered. The sun glinted off her bejeweled purple robes, but her smile was the brightest thing in the room.

However, it soon became clear that Padmé

still saw Anakin as the little boy she had met on the desert planet Tatooine all those years before. Anakin's heart fell, and Padmé turned to the matter at hand.

"I don't need more security," Padmé told the two Jedi. "I need answers. I want to know who's trying to kill me."

"We are here to protect you, Senator, not start an investigation," Obi-Wan reminded her.

But Anakin longed to reassure her. He leaned forward and said, "We *will* find out who's trying to kill you, Padmé. I promise."

Obi-Wan bristled—both from the thought of going against the Jedi Council's strict orders and from surprise at hearing his apprentice speak out of turn.

"We will not exceed our mandate, my young Padawan learner."

A beat of tense silence ensued. Anakin wanted to argue. He longed to prove himself, to Padmé *and* Obi-Wan—but the senator was as diplomatic as ever.

"Perhaps with merely your presence, the mystery surrounding this threat will be revealed," she said politely as she swept out of the room.

That evening, Anakin and Obi-Wan guarded the senator's chambers while Padmé slept.

Suddenly, Anakin jerked his head up.

"I sense it, too," Obi-Wan assured him.

The Jedi charged into Padmé's room and Anakin leapt onto her bed, igniting his lightsaber—the weapon of a Jedi Knight—to destroy two venomous kouhuns that were about to bite the senator. The lethal millipedes were flung against the wall as Padmé awoke with a gasp.

But just outside her window, the courier droid that had delivered the kouhuns was about to disappear.

Without a moment's hesitation, Obi-Wan jumped out of the window, crashing through the glass and latching on to the machine as it sped away through the lanes of heavy traffic that crisscrossed Coruscant's night sky.

"Stay here!" Anakin told Padmé. He hurried outside and leapt into an awaiting speeder, tuning into the Force—the energy field that connected all living things—to track his master through the hustle and bustle. It was a good thing Anakin's abilities were so honed, as a mysterious figure shot a blast at the courier droid, causing Obi-Wan to plummet through the traffic in a freefall.

Anakin maneuvered the speeder under Obi-Wan, catching his master handily.

The assassin led them on a chaotic chase as Obi-Wan held on for dear life — he was not fond of Anakin's aggressive piloting.

Suddenly, Anakin stopped the speeder altogether and jumped out, into a freefall of his own!

The young Jedi would have seemed crazy had he not landed on top of the assassin's speeder, exactly as he had planned. Anakin stabbed his lightsaber into the cockpit, cutting off all control, and the ship crashed to the street below and slid to a halt.

The assassin leapt out and ran, but it was no use — the Jedi soon cornered the woman: a shape-shifting Clawdite. However, before the assassin could tell them who had hired her to kill the senator, a toxic dart plunged into her neck, killing *her*.

The next day, Obi-Wan and Anakin stood before the Jedi High Council. The Jedi Masters ordered Obi-Wan to track the deadly dart's origins to discover who had hired the assassin while Anakin escorted Padmé back to Naboo, where she would be safe.

Chancellor Palpatine was also anxious to see Padmé return home with Anakin as her guard. The older man had always encouraged the young Jedi.

"I have said it many times: You are the most gifted Jedi I have ever met," the Chancellor told Anakin. "I see you becoming the greatest of all the Jedi, Anakin, even more powerful than Master Yoda."

Hearing such words from Palpatine filled Anakin's heart with pride, and he was thrilled to have the opportunity to escort Padmé to her home planet.

But as Padmé packed her bags, she told Anakin that she didn't want to leave Coruscant. Some members of the Senate were pushing to give Chancellor Palpatine special powers to create an army of the Republic, but Padmé had worked for a year to oppose the amendment and she did not want to risk leaving if there was to be a vote soon.

"Sometimes we must let go of our pride and do what is requested of us," Anakin told her.

Padmé stopped packing to give him a nod of approval. "Anakin, you've grown up."

"Master Obi-Wan manages not to see it," he confided.

Padmé could sense Anakin's frustration.

"Our mentors have a way of seeing more of our faults than we would like," she said matter-of-factly. "It's the only way we grow."

Anakin sat down on the bed, head hanging. "I know."

Padmé stepped near, finally looking at him. "Anakin. Don't try to grow up too fast."

He stood, towering over her, and stared deeply into her eyes. "But I *am* grown-up. You said it yourself."

Padmé stepped away. "Please don't look at me like that."

"Why not?"

"It makes me feel uncomfortable," she said curtly, shaking off the closeness she had let herself feel between them and turning back to her packing—taking refuge, as always, in the task at hand.

"Sorry, m'lady," he said with a smile, knowing she was not being entirely truthful.

Soon Anakin and Padmé, dressed in disguise as common refugees, boarded an unregistered transport ship along with their faithful droid, R2-D2. As they shared a meal on board the ship — not as a former queen and a Jedi-in-training but as just two ordinary people — Padmé let herself engage more with Anakin.

"It must be difficult, having sworn your life to the Jedi. Not being able to visit the places you like or do the things you like."

"Or be with the people I love," Anakin said.

Padmé shook her head, taken aback once again by his boldness.

"Are you allowed to love?" she asked, almost as a challenge. "I thought that was forbidden to the Jedi."

Anakin struggled for the right words, words that were true to the Jedi code but also true to his own feelings.

"Attachment is forbidden. Possession is forbidden. Compassion, which I would define as unconditional love, is central to a Jedi's life. So you might say that we are encouraged to love," the young Jedi explained with a grin.

Padmé found herself smiling in return. She was surprised by Anakin's charm.

"You've changed so much," she murmured.

"You haven't changed a bit," Anakin replied. He sensed their growing closeness and started to allow himself to hope that their friendship might turn into something deeper.

Meanwhile, Obi-Wan worked to track down whoever had hired Padmé's would-be assassin. When he took the assassin's dart to his old friend, Dexter Jettster, a jolly four-armed Besalisk who owned a diner on Coruscant, Dex told Obi-Wan that the dart was from Kamino, a planet whose people were known for their prowess at cloning. But Obi-Wan could not find Kamino on the Jedi Temple's star chart. It seemed as though the planet did not exist.

Obi-Wan asked Master Yoda about the missing planet, and Yoda shook his head.

"Lost a planet, Master Obi-Wan has," he told his youngling class. "How embarrassing!"

The little ones giggled, but one wise child spoke up. "Master, someone erased it from the archive memory."

Yoda chuckled. "Truly wonderful, the mind of a child is," he said. "The Padawan is right. Go to the center of gravity's pull, and find your planet you will."

Anakin and Padmé soon landed on Naboo and sought refuge in the remote Lake Country, where Padmé would be safest. It was beautiful there, with glimmering blue lakes and emerald green hills.

"We used to come here for school retreat," Padmé told Anakin as they walked along a stone balcony. Confiding in him had become easier along their journey.

Anakin felt so close to her in that moment that he reached out to touch her hand. Padmé turned to him, looking up into his eyes, and the two shared a kiss.

But Padmé suddenly pulled away.

"I shouldn't have done that," she said.

Anakin apologized. He knew Padmé was confused about her feelings for him. He was confused, too. As much as he may have tried to convince himself otherwise, he knew romantic relationships were forbidden under the Jedi

Order—and being a Jedi had always been Anakin's dream. But with Padmé, he found himself wanting more.

Still, Anakin and Padmé spent every day together, talking and laughing and exploring the countryside. Their feelings for each other only grew deeper.

One night, as they sat by the fire together, Anakin could stay silent no longer.

"From the moment I met you, all those years ago, not a day has gone by that I haven't thought of you," he told Padmé.

"We can't. It's just not possible," Padmé replied, shaking her head. "If you follow your thoughts through to conclusion, it'll take us to a place we cannot go, regardless of the way we feel about each other."

Anakin's heart swelled, knowing that Padmé shared his feelings.

"I will not let you give up your future for me," she added.

"It wouldn't have to be that way," Anakin suggested, desperate for a solution. "We could keep it a secret."

"We'd be living a lie, one we couldn't keep even if we wanted to." Padmé sighed.

"No, you're right," Anakin said, tearing his eyes away from her. "It would destroy us."

That night, something else almost destroyed Anakin. He had a troubling vision about his mother, Shmi, who'd stayed behind on Tatooine when he'd left with Qui-Gon Jinn to train as a Jedi. Anakin sensed that she was in trouble; he felt her suffering and knew she was in pain.

Although it would be disobeying his mandate to protect Padmé, he simply had to go find his mother and help her. Padmé knew a relationship with Anakin was forbidden, but she understood his need to find his mother and she wanted to help. She decided to go with him to Tatooine.

Across the galaxy, Obi-Wan landed his starship amid a raging storm on the watery planet Kamino. There he was greeted by tall, soft-spoken aliens, who explained that a grand clone army had long before been ordered by Jedi Master Sifo-Dyas on behalf of the Galactic Senate — and that the army was almost ready.

The aliens took Obi-Wan through their massive facilities, and the Jedi watched in awe as thousands upon thousands of humans, all the exact same height with the exact same features, worked and trained in unison.

When Obi-Wan asked to meet the genetic donor from whom the clones were created, he was introduced to a bounty hunter named Jango Fett and his son, Boba, one of the unaltered clones. During their tense conversation, Obi-Wan sensed he had found the mastermind behind the attempts on Padmé's life, but he waited to discuss his suspicions in a holochat with Mace Windu and Yoda back on Coruscant.

The Jedi Masters confirmed that they had no knowledge of a Jedi-ordered clone army, and it was presumed that Jedi Master Sifo-Dyas had died many years earlier. It was all a great mystery, but Mace Windu and Yoda urged Obi-Wan to bring Jango Fett back to Coruscant for questioning so they could get to the bottom of things.

Unfortunately, Jango Fett knew the Jedi had recognized him, so he made preparations to escape Kamino with Boba in their large ship, *Slave I*.

Obi-Wan refused to let the bounty hunter go so easily and engaged the armored mercenary in battle.

Although he didn't have Force powers or a lightsaber, Jango was a skilled warrior with plenty of tricks up his sleeve. As Boba primed their ship, Jango fought the Jedi with rockets, blasters, and a grappling line, dragging Obi-Wan through the rain and nearly landing them both in the monster-riddled seas below.

Jango and his son managed to escape — but not before Obi-Wan tossed a homing beacon onto their ship's hull.

Landing on the hot sands of his home planet, Anakin learned that Shmi had married a moisture farmer named Cliegg Lars, who had rescued her from the life of slavery Anakin had shared before he'd left to become a Jedi.

When Anakin and Padmé arrived at the Lars farm, they were greeted by an old friend: C-3PO, the protocol droid Anakin had built as a boy!

"Oh, Master Ani! I knew you would return. And Miss Padmé!" C-3PO shouted, recognizing them in spite of the decade that had passed. "Bless my circuits, I'm so pleased to see you both."

But Anakin soon learned from Cliegg that his mother had been kidnapped by Tusken Raiders.

"Those Tuskens walk like men, but they're vicious, mindless monsters," Cliegg said. "Thirty of us went out after her. Four of us came back. I don't want to give up on her, but she's been gone a month. There's little hope she's lasted this long."

Anakin stood.

"Where are you going?" Cliegg's son, Owen, asked.

"To find my mother," Anakin told him.

Hopping on a rusty old speeder bike, Anakin took off across the desert. As the twin suns set, hot and red, he just hoped he wouldn't be too late.

Three moons shone full and white as Anakin watched the Tusken Raider camp from a plateau high above. Two dozen circular tents glowed red with firelight. Calling on the Force, Anakin jumped to the ground, landed in a run, and swiftly found the tent where his mother was tied up, bruised and beaten.

"Ani?" she said, barely able to speak. "Is it you?"

He released her bindings and held her. "I'm here, Mom. You're safe."

"Ani? Oh, you look so handsome. My son. Oh, my grown-up son," Shmi said with what little energy she had left. "I'm so proud of you, Ani."

She cupped his face, and he kissed her palm.

"I missed you," he whispered.

She struggled to speak. "Now I am complete. I love y— "

But she was too hurt to go on.

Shmi fell back in Anakin's arms, and Anakin felt her death. It happened so quickly, with just a breath, and yet it hit him harder than anything he could ever have imagined.

If only he'd come sooner. He had failed her, his beloved mother who'd given everything for him.

But as he held her in the orange firelight, his guilt transformed into fury. Her death was not his fault.

It was *theirs*.

Anakin closed his mother's eyes and gently lay her body on the ground.

He stepped out of the tent and ignited his

lightsaber. Blinded by rage, Anakin showed no mercy to the Tusken Raiders.

For what they had done to his mother, Anakin slaughtered the entire encampment.

Obi-Wan had no idea what his Padawan had done. He was following the Jedi Council's orders and tracking Jango Fett through space.

The bounty hunter, however, soon discovered that he was being followed and began to fire on the Jedi's starship. *Slave I* blasted through an asteroid field, detonating deadly seismic charges that shattered everything in their wake with waves of brilliant blue light.

Obi-Wan dodged the crumbling asteroids that flew through the darkness of space around his ship. When Jango fired a homing missile at the Jedi, Obi-Wan quickly ordered his astromech droid, R4-P17, to release spare parts from their ship for the missile to hit instead as he landed on a large asteroid to stay out of sight.

As he entered the atmosphere of a rocky world known as Geonosis, Jango believed he had defeated Obi-Wan once and for all. But the Jedi simply lay in wait and then surreptitiously followed *Slave I* down to the planet's surface. Obi-Wan had to learn who was really behind the attempt on Padmé's life . . . and the strange army of clones.

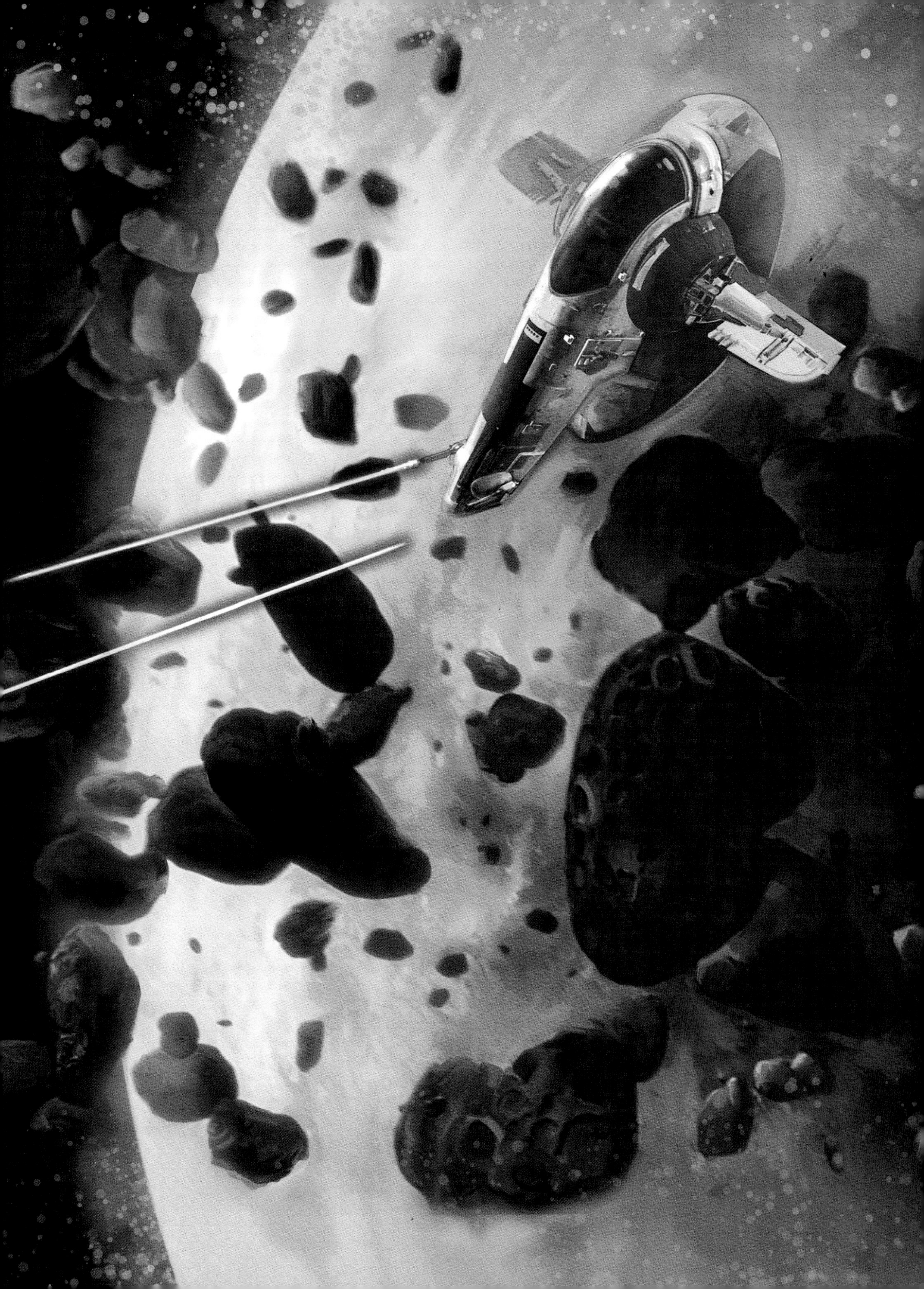

On Tatooine, Anakin took his mother's body back to the Lars farm.

"Why'd she have to die?" Anakin asked Padmé, fighting tears. "Why couldn't I save her?"

"Sometimes there are things no one can fix," she told him gently. "You're not all-powerful, Ani."

"Well, I should be," Anakin replied, still too full of emotion to think clearly. "Someday I will be. I will be the most powerful Jedi ever! I promise you. I will even learn to stop people from dying."

"Anakin!" Padmé stopped him from going further. This was not the little boy she had befriended years before, and it was not the young man she had grown so close to in recent weeks.

Anakin crumpled under his pain and guilt.

He admitted to Padmé that he had killed the Tusken Raiders.

But instead of stepping back in fear or disgust, Padmé knelt beside him on the floor.

"To be angry is to be human," she said.

"I'm a Jedi. I know I'm better than this."

Later, as Anakin stood before Shmi's grave on the small family farm, he swore an oath to her and to himself.

"I wasn't strong enough to save you, Mom. But I promise I won't fail again."

Suddenly, R2 showed up from Anakin and Padmé's ship with a message from Obi-Wan. The Jedi, who still believed his Padawan to be on Naboo, needed Anakin to transmit his message to Coruscant, letting the Jedi Masters know that he had tracked Jango Fett to a Separatist base on Geonosis.

There, Obi-Wan had learned that an old enemy, the Trade Federation's Viceroy Gunray, was ultimately behind the attempt on Senator Amidala's life. Along with the Trade Federation, other factions – the Commerce Guild and the Corporate Alliance – had pledged their droid armies to the leader of the Separatists, a former Jedi named Count Dooku. But Obi-Wan's transmission abruptly cut off as a heavily shielded droideka appeared and started to attack the Jedi as he was recording the message.

"We will deal with Count Dooku," the Jedi High Council told Anakin from across the galaxy. "The most important thing is for you to stay where you are. Protect the senator at all costs."

But Padmé convinced Anakin that the Jedi Council would never get to Geonosis in time to save Obi-Wan. She and Anakin, however, were less than a parsec away.

"Ani, are you just going to sit here and let him die?" Padmé asked. "He's your friend, your mentor. He's – "

"He's like my father," Anakin agreed. "But you heard Master Windu. He gave me strict orders to stay here."

"He gave you strict orders to *protect me*," Padmé shot back, already powering up their ship. "And I'm going to help Obi-Wan. If you plan to protect me, you'll just have to come along."

As soon as Anakin and Padmé landed on Geonosis, they were attacked by insectile Geonosian soldiers and had to sneak into a droid-making factory to seek refuge. Inside the factory was no safer, however. As molten metal poured from large vats and mechanical conveyer belts ferried in-process droids this way and that, the two young friends tried to make their way through the complicated mess of machinery.

C-3PO and R2, who had followed their masters, likewise ended up in the foundry, with the protocol droid accidentally exchanging his head with a droid soldier while R2 flew out of danger using hidden repulsors.

Suddenly, Jango Fett appeared in front of them, with a fleet of droidekas to surround them. Anakin's lightsaber had been damaged during the ordeal, so they had no choice but to surrender.

"Don't be afraid," Anakin told Padmé as they stood together in shackles, awaiting their fate.

"I'm not afraid to die." She looked into his eyes. "I've been dying a little bit each day since you came back into my life."

Anakin couldn't believe what he'd just heard. "What are you talking about?"

"I love you."

Hearing those words . . . changed everything.

It was as if Anakin's heart cracked wide open, as if he could breathe for the first time after ten years of holding his breath.

"You love me? I thought we had decided not to fall in love. That we would be forced to live a lie, and that it would destroy our lives."

"Anakin, I think our lives are about to be destroyed anyway. I truly, deeply love you, and before we die, I want you to know."

And then they kissed, even as a chariot pulled them into the harsh, carved-rock stadium where they would meet their fate.

Millions of insectile Geonosians cheered and chittered their excitement at the promise of watching an execution.

Obi-Wan was already chained to a pillar in the arena.

"I was beginning to wonder if you'd got my message," he said to Anakin.

A soldier attached Anakin's manacles to a chain, pinning him to another stone pillar as the Padawan told Obi-Wan, "I retransmitted it just as you had requested, Master. Then we decided to come and rescue you."

"Good job," Obi-Wan said, his voice dripping with sarcasm, as Padmé was chained to a third pillar.

Far overhead on a dais, Geonosian leader Poggle the Lesser spoke to the crowds in his language of clicks: "Let the execution begin!"

By his side stood Count Dooku, as well as Jango and Boba Fett.

The crowd went wild as three beasts were released into the arena. The first was a four-legged reek, its pebbled skin bright red with a meaty luster and its three horns ready to tear any prey to shreds. Next came an acklay, a vicious green creature with six deadly claws and a mouth full of fangs. Last came a nexu, a four-eyed predator with razor-sharp teeth and a spray of sharp quills across its back. The bloodthirsty nexu immediately took out a Geonosian guard.

"I've got a bad feeling about this," Anakin said.

But he didn't notice Padmé using a hairpin she'd hidden in her mouth to unlock her manacles. She began to climb her stone pillar as the three monstrous beasts were driven forward by guards.

The acklay went for Obi-Wan, attempting to stab him with a sharp claw. But Obi-Wan used the acklay's own attack to slice through his chain, leaving him free to run. When the reek tried to ram Anakin with its center horn, the young Jedi flipped over the creature's head and landed on its back, using the horn to snap his chain. The agile nexu climbed the pillar toward Padmé, but she slashed it across the face with her chain. In return, it raked her back with its claws as it fell to the ground.

Anakin was astride the reek, struggling to stay on its sloped back. Unable to hold on, he fell and held his chain as he was dragged behind the rampaging beast. Using his Force powers on the reek, Anakin leapt onto its back again and steered it to ram and kill the nexu. High above, Padmé jumped down and landed behind Anakin on the reek, wrapping her arms tightly around his waist and quickly kissing him on the cheek.

Meanwhile, Obi-Wan was fighting off both the furious acklay and a hoard of Geonosian guards, using only a stolen spear. When Anakin steered the reek toward him, Obi-Wan jumped up behind Padmé.

But just when it seemed like the three friends had survived their execution sentence, droidekas rolled in from every side, surrounding them. Without any weapon except a half-tamed reek, Anakin could not see a way out. . . .

Suddenly, all around the stands, the telltale glow of lightsabers lit the arena. The Jedi had arrived! The Geonosians escaped on fluttering wings as Mace Windu faced the aged but powerful Count Dooku on the dais.

As if on cue, a droid army marched into view, wasting no time in aiming their blasters at the Jedi. But the Jedi were unafraid. They leapt as one into the stadium, running toward the droids with lightsabers ready, deflecting blaster bolts to strike down the droid soldiers. The Jedi threw spare lightsabers to Anakin and Obi-Wan, and Padmé picked up a fallen blaster to join the fight, as well.

Padmé leapt onto one of the Geonosian

mounts, a reptilian orray, and Anakin hopped into the chariot it pulled. Together, they cut a swath through the droids, leaving a trail of smoking metal behind them.

When their orray was killed by a droideka, Anakin and Padmé were hurled onto the sand. Weapon in hand, Padmé took shelter in the fallen chariot as Anakin defended her. They watched as Obi-Wan killed the acklay that had nearly ended him.

C-3PO, trapped under a droid soldier, was rescued and reunited with his proper body by the canny R2, who always seemed to show up just in the nick of time.

But despite their brave fighting, the Jedi were surrounded and outnumbered by droids.

"Master Windu, you have fought gallantly," Count Dooku intoned from his safe place on the dais. "But now it is finished. Surrender, and your lives will be spared."

"We will not be hostages to be bartered, Dooku," Mace said.

"Then I'm sorry, old friend."

The droids' blasters clicked into place, and the Jedi valiantly raised their weapons, ready to fight to the end.

"Look!" cried Padmé, pointing to the sky.

A fleet of transport ships descended from above, led by Master Yoda. Each ship was filled with identical soldiers ready for battle!

Back on Coruscant, the Senate had given Chancellor Palpatine special powers, which he'd used to take possession of the army of clones developed on Kamino. The clone army was still shrouded in mystery, but it was certainly needed.

The ships created a ring around the Jedi, holding off the droid army with their massive firepower. Anakin helped Padmé into one of the transports as the Jedi fought their way to safety, pulling each other into the ships as the clones protected them from the droids.

The ships blasted off, but the battle was far from over. Outside the arena, Count Dooku unleashed the full fury of his combined droid armies and Trade Federation starships. Mace and Yoda took control of the clone army, putting it to work against the enemy's weapons.

Little did they know that deep inside the Geonosian palace, Poggle the Lesser had decided to retreat.

"The Jedi must not find our designs for the ultimate weapon," he told Count Dooku. "If they find out what we are planning to build, we're doomed."

"I will take the designs with me to Coruscant," Dooku said, holding the holo of a spherical, moonlike weapon — the Death Star. "They will be much safer there with my master."

Dooku took off on a speeder bike across the surface of the planet, but Obi-Wan spotted him from their ship. Dooku's guards landed a shot

on the Jedi transport, knocking Padmé into the dunes far below. Anakin wanted to save her, but Obi-Wan stopped him.

"I can't take Dooku alone. I need you. If we catch him, we can end this war right now! We have a job to do!" Obi-Wan shouted.

"I don't care!" Anakin shouted back. "Put the ship down!"

"Come to your senses! What do you think Padmé would do were she in your position?"

Anakin was breathing heard, his heart pounding. But he knew Obi-Wan was right. "She would do her duty," he said, head hanging, unable to meet his master's eyes.

Dooku's speeder slipped into a cavern on the side of a mountain, and Anakin and Obi-Wan leapt out of their ship to follow him.

When Anakin and Obi-Wan cornered the former Jedi, their lightsabers drawn, Count Dooku calmly turned to them, his own custom lightsaber visible on his belt.

"You're going to pay for all the Jedi you killed today, Dooku," Anakin said.

"We'll take him together. Go in slowly on the left," Obi-Wan directed.

But Anakin was done waiting.

"I'm taking him now!" he growled, running at Dooku.

"No, Anakin!" Obi-Wan shouted.

But it was too late. Count Dooku raised his hand and Force lightning sprang forth, enrobing Anakin in electricity and slamming him into a stone wall. Anakin was stunned. Every nerve was on fire, and his Jedi robes were smoking from the blast.

Obi-Wan circled Dooku, who still hadn't drawn his lightsaber.

"As you can see, my Jedi powers are far beyond yours," the older man said. "Now, back down."

He raised his hand and sent more lightning at Obi-Wan. But the younger Jedi coolly absorbed the power using his lightsaber and merely said, "I don't think so."

Hearing that, Dooku finally lit his own lightsaber, which glowed bright red. When the duel began, Anakin couldn't believe Dooku could fight with such energy and grace, leaping and dodging like a man a quarter of his age. Obi-Wan fought furiously but was still failing. And then, looking disappointed with the younger Jedi, Dooku grazed Obi-Wan's arm and leg with his lightsaber, and Anakin's master fell.

As Dooku raised his red lightsaber for a final stroke against Obi-Wan, Anakin summoned all his power and used the Force to leap across the room, blocking the blade as Obi-Wan lay helpless.

"Brave of you, boy," Dooku said blandly. "I would've thought you'd learned your lesson."

"I'm a slow learner," Anakin sneered.

Just then, Obi-Wan used the Force to throw his lightsaber directly into Anakin's other hand, and Anakin ignited it, dueling the great Count Dooku with two blades.

Dooku slashed one lightsaber hilt, and the blade sputtered out, leaving Anakin with a single weapon again. He leapt back and sliced a power cable, and lights began to flicker on and off. It was like a dance as he battled the powerful Count Dooku, who had once been master to Anakin's early mentor, Jedi Knight Qui-Gon Jinn, before leaving the Jedi Order.

Anakin relished testing his skills and felt the Force flow through him, but then Dooku took him completely by surprise. He whipped his lightsaber around and sliced off Anakin's right arm at the elbow! The lightsaber's heat cauterized the wound, sealing it as Anakin landed beside Obi-Wan on the ground, writhing in pain.

Anakin had to be dreaming, he thought as he saw Master Yoda hobbling into the chamber using his cane.

"Master Yoda," Dooku said.

"Count Dooku," Yoda replied.

"You have interfered with our affairs for the last time."

Using his Force powers, Count Dooku threw a heavy piece of metal at Yoda, but Yoda used his own powers to toss it aside. Again and again, Dooku tried to crush the small, ancient alien, even bringing down part of the ceiling.

"Powerful you have become, Dooku. The dark side I sense in you," Yoda observed.

"I've become more powerful than any Jedi. Even you," Dooku shot back as he raised his hand to throw lightning at Yoda. But Yoda didn't flinch. He didn't even draw his lightsaber. He merely caught the lightning in his hand and sent it right back at Dooku, who redirected it into the ceiling with a terrific crash.

"Much to learn, you still have," Yoda said sadly.

Dooku drew his lightsaber. "It is obvious

that this contest cannot be decided by our knowledge of the Force . . . but by our skills with a lightsaber."

Dooku ignited his red blade, and Yoda lit his green blade, the entire apparatus as small as the youngling weapons Anakin had handled so long before.

It was beautiful and terrifying as the two battled – one for good, the other for evil. Their blades, green and red, flared as they flipped acrobatically around the chamber.

"Fought well you have, my old Padawan," Yoda said.

"This is just the beginning," Dooku snarled. He used the Force to pull down a huge piece of machinery that hovered over Anakin and Obi-Wan, who lay helpless, unable to move. Yoda was forced to choose. He could either pursue Dooku as he escaped or save Anakin and Obi-Wan, who were about to be crushed.

Closing his eyes, Yoda stopped the falling metal as Dooku shot into the air in a spaceship, eluding the clone troopers' blasts.

The fight was over. Yoda hung his lightsaber on his belt as Padmé ran in, too late to help.

They had lost.

Sometime later, in a secret faraway place, Dooku's ship landed in a red-lit hangar. A black-robed figure approached him.

"The Force is with us, Master Sidious," Dooku said.

"Welcome home, Lord Tyranus. You have done well," the figure responded.

"I have good news for you, my lord. The war has begun."

The evil Sith Lord Darth Sidious nodded.

"Excellent. Everything is going as planned."

Chancellor Palpatine looked on as the Galactic Republic's new army of clones filed into ships. They would be transported across the galaxy, to fight the Separatists and regain peace.

But in the Jedi Council Chambers, Yoda hung his head as he spoke with Mace and Obi-Wan.

"The shroud of the dark side has fallen. Begun, the Clone War has."

But on Naboo, there was still hope. As the sun set over the lake where they'd first kissed, Anakin and Padmé joined hands in marriage. It would be their secret, they'd agreed, so R2 and C-3PO were their only witnesses. Anakin took Padmé's hand in his new prosthetic metal fingers and kissed her gently. He had dreamed of freedom and then aspired to become a Jedi, but in truth, Padmé was the beginning and the end of his world.

And he would do anything to keep her safe.

REVENGE OF THE SITH

A galaxy at war . . .

The fighting between the democratic Galactic Republic and an evil faction known as the Separatists seemed unending. The Jedi—an ancient order of noble protectors—fought alongside the clone army of the Republic to battle back the Separatists' droid militia.

Led by the powerful fallen Jedi Count Dooku and the maniacal cyborg General Grievous, the Separatists kidnapped the leader of the Republic, Chancellor Palpatine. But the factious group had even darker ties than the Jedi or the Republic could imagine. Count Dooku had pledged his loyalty to the shadowy Sith Lord Darth Sidious. Yet the real identity of Darth Sidious, and his true motive, remained a mystery.

However, one talented Jedi Knight, Anakin Skywalker, who was secretly wed to a Republic senator, Padmé Amidala, was soon to uncover the truth. . . .

Jedi Knights Anakin Skywalker and Obi-Wan Kenobi flew their starfighters directly for General Grievous's ship, dodging enemy fire on their mission to save the leader of the Galactic Senate, Chancellor Palpatine, who had been kidnapped by the Separatist cyborg warrior.

Anakin had trained under Obi-Wan, but the student now far outflew the teacher. With massive battlecruisers hanging in space and a riot of vulture droids trying to blast them out of the sky, Anakin and his trusty astromech, R2-D2, helped Obi-Wan fight off a squad of pesky buzz droids before the two Jedi skidded their starfighters into the hangar of the general's command ship.

"Oh, I have a bad feeling about this," Obi-Wan said.

Leaping out of their ships, they battled dozens of droid soldiers with their lightsabers, then followed R2 toward the location of the Chancellor's distress beacon.

"I sense Count Dooku," Anakin said, remembering well his past duel with the fallen Jedi and leader of the Separatists, who was now steeped in the dark side of the Force.

"I sense a trap," Obi-Wan corrected him.

"Next move?"

Obi-Wan grinned. "Spring the trap!"

The two Jedi fought past droidekas and an entire lift filled with confused B1 battle droids before they found the kidnapped Chancellor sitting stiffly in a command chair.

"Count Dooku," Palpatine warned them.

As if on cue, Count Dooku appeared behind the Jedi, flanked by B2 battle droids.

"This time we will do it together," Obi-Wan told Anakin.

"I was about to say that."

Last time, Anakin had run right at Dooku, and for that arrogance he'd lost his right hand.

Dooku flipped from an upper balcony to the floor and calmly drew his lightsaber.

"Get help," Palpatine whispered. "You're no match for him. He's a Sith Lord."

Obi-Wan turned to the older man with a charming grin. "Chancellor Palpatine, Sith Lords are our specialty."

All three lightsabers flared to life at once as they each attempted a strike, testing one another.

"I've been looking forward to this," Count Dooku said with an eager grin.

Anakin stepped forward, his mechanical fist clenched around his saber. "My powers have doubled since the last time we met, Count."

"Good. Twice the pride, double the fall."

They dueled again, and Count Dooku used the Force to throw Obi-Wan to the ground as he battled Anakin up the stairs. But every time Anakin gained ground or Obi-Wan rejoined the fight, Dooku used another dirty trick, finally Force-choking Obi-Wan, tossing him off the balcony, and calling on the dark side of the Force to bring down a piece of decking to pin the Jedi.

Anakin's rage coursed through him. He advanced on the Count, his lightsaber catching the older man's weapon and bringing Anakin face to face with Dooku.

"I sense great fear in you, Skywalker," Dooku goaded. "You have hate. You have anger. But you don't use them."

Anakin said nothing, just doubled his efforts to win the duel. Their sabers struck again and again, and Anakin fought to control the very emotions Count Dooku had tried to bring to the surface. Finally, he found his Jedi calm, and with one swift stroke, he sliced off Count Dooku's hands at the wrists and caught the Sith's lit red lightsaber midair.

"Good, Anakin. Good," Chancellor Palpatine called as Anakin held the two lightsabers, one twitch away from ending Count Dooku forever.

"Kill him," Palpatine urged. "Kill him now."

Anakin's hands shook. His feelings and the Chancellor both urged him to end the Sith Lord, but his Jedi training told him not to.

"I shouldn't."

Count Dooku was breathing hard, looking every year of his age, finally powerless.

"Do it," Palpatine growled.

Anakin only hesitated for a moment before following the Chancellor's command. But the moment after it was done, he questioned himself. Master Yoda and Master Windu — leaders of the Jedi Order — would not approve. But wasn't it a good thing to stop a Sith Lord?

"You did well, Anakin," Palpatine told him. "He was too dangerous to be kept alive."

"Yes, but he was an unarmed prisoner. I shouldn't have done that. It's not the Jedi way." Anakin released Palpatine's restraints, allowing the older man to stand.

"It is only natural. He cut off your arm, and you wanted revenge. It wasn't the first time, Anakin. Remember what you told me about your mother and the Sand People?"

The memory of Anakin's past furies stung in the young Jedi's mind.

"Now we must leave before more security droids arrive," Palpatine concluded.

Anakin ran to Obi-Wan, pulling him out from under the fallen balcony, but Palpatine tried to stop him. "Leave him, or we'll never make it."

But Obi-Wan was Anakin's closest friend. He would never leave his master behind.

"His fate will be the same as ours," Anakin told the Chancellor, carrying Obi-Wan over his shoulder.

Their escape was not easy, and Obi-Wan woke up just in time to be captured by General Grievous's droids.

"That wasn't much of a rescue," General Grievous gasped. The cyborg was feared throughout the galaxy for his hunting prowess and strategic genius, but transforming his body into a fighting machine had left his organic anatomy weak inside his armor.

"General Grievous. You're shorter than I expected," Anakin countered.

"Jedi scum," Grievous wheezed between coughing fits.

General Grievous stripped the Jedi of their lightsabers. But Anakin gave R2 a signal, and the little droid created a diversion, shooting electricity and beeping madly. In the chaos, R2 freed the Jedi from their manacles and provided Anakin and Obi-Wan with hidden lightsabers.

The Jedi fought past the general's battle droids to free Palpatine and then focused on Grievous himself.

"You won't get away this time," Obi-Wan told him.

But General Grievous surprised them by stabbing the cockpit glass and letting the cold vacuum of space suck him outside, where they couldn't reach him. Anakin and Obi-Wan struggled to hold on until the cockpit resealed, but Grievous had already disappeared.

They had no choice but to make a dangerous emergency landing on Coruscant, thanks again to Anakin's impressive piloting skills.

Back on Coruscant, the Galactic Senate voted to continue the war as long as the dastardly General Grievous was still alive, and the Jedi High Council therefore decided that killing Grievous was their highest priority. As for Anakin, he just wanted to see his wife, Padmé Amidala, a senator and longtime friend whom he had wed in secret – going against the rules of the Jedi Order.

"Something wonderful has happened," Padmé told Anakin. "I'm pregnant."

For a second, Anakin didn't know what to think. He was elated, but how would they continue to hide their relationship from the world so he could still play his part as a Jedi? He pushed all such thoughts from his mind; they would find a way to be together.

"That's wonderful," he told her. "This is the happiest moment of my life."

But soon Anakin was having terrible visions of Padmé struggling during childbirth, screaming and begging him for help. They were so similar to other haunting visions he'd had in the past – visions that had turned out to be true – that he could only see them as Force visions of the future. Fear of losing Padmé festered and swelled inside him, unlike anything he had ever felt before.

He touched the necklace he had made for Padmé so long before, when he was just a small boy on Tatooine. Now it hung just above Padmé's growing belly.

Even back then, Anakin had known how much he loved her, how much he needed her.

"It was only a dream," Padmé assured him.

"I won't let this one become real."

Anakin couldn't wait to be a father, but he had to keep Padmé alive no matter what.

Seeking advice about his visions, Anakin first went to Master Yoda, but it was hard for him to speak openly while still concealing his secret relationship with Padmé.

"Careful you must be when sensing the future, Anakin," Yoda warned. "The fear of loss is a path to the dark side. You must train yourself to let go of everything you fear to lose."

Anakin left feeling just as unsettled. Letting go of Padmé was simply not an option.

Anakin did not think he should confide in Obi-Wan, either, even though they were closer than brothers. Obi-Wan was still part of the Jedi Order, and Anakin felt that the Jedi laws were the cause of his current predicament.

So Anakin went to see Chancellor Palpatine. The leader of the Republic had always encouraged the young Jedi and praised him for his talents.

But before Anakin could bring up his concerns, something unexpected happened: Chancellor Palpatine informed Anakin that he was to join the Jedi Council as Palpatine's personal representative.

Anakin was eager to prove himself and make the Chancellor proud, but he sensed that the Jedi Masters on the Council would not welcome him as an equal. Despite his advanced skills and power in the ways of the Force, Anakin knew he was still seen as too young and immature.

The Jedi leaders agreed to invite Anakin to be a member of the Council, however they were clear in telling him that he would not be given the traditional rank of Jedi Master.

"What? How can you do this?" Anakin asked. "This is outrageous."

Anakin was disappointed that the Jedi had done just as he had expected: they'd treated him like a child.

To make matters worse, Obi-Wan told him later that the Jedi leaders had only agreed to have Anakin on the Council because they felt it was an opportunity for him to spy on the Chancellor. Some of the Jedi were unsure of Palpatine's motives.

Anakin was aghast.

"You're asking me to do something against the Jedi code! Against the Republic, against a mentor and a friend. Why are you asking this of me?"

"The *Council* is asking you," Obi-Wan said, trying to reassure his friend of the Jedi Order's good intentions.

But Anakin was starting to question the Jedi Order. By their code, he was not allowed to be with the woman he loved or have the child who would soon come into the world. But they were asking him to spy on a friend and to surreptitiously challenge the Republic, which seemed far more dangerous than his attachment to Padmé.

Anakin's head was spinning. Nothing seemed to make sense anymore.

That night, Chancellor Palpatine invited Anakin to join him at the opera, and Anakin shared his doubts with the older man.

"All who gain power are afraid to lose it. Even the Jedi," Palpatine told him sadly.

"But the Jedi use their power for good," Anakin argued.

The Chancellor sighed. "Good is a point of view, Anakin. The Sith and the Jedi are similar in almost every way, including their quest for greater power."

For a moment, they watched the show, with ribbons of color rippling through glowing bubbles of swirling light. Then Palpatine asked, "Did you ever hear the tragedy of Darth Plagueis the Wise?"

The Sith name alone revolted Anakin. "No."

"I thought not. It's not a story the Jedi would tell you. It's a Sith legend. Darth Plagueis was a dark lord of the Sith so powerful and so wise he could use the Force to create life. He had such a knowledge of the dark side, he could even keep the ones he cared about from dying."

Palpatine gave Anakin a significant, pitying look, as if he could see straight through to Anakin's darkest fears of losing Padmé.

"He could actually . . . save people from death?" Anakin asked.

Palpatine faced forward as he spoke. "The dark side of the Force is a pathway to many abilities some consider to be . . . unnatural."

Anakin couldn't stop himself from asking, "What happened to him?"

"He became so powerful the only thing he was afraid of was . . . losing his power. Which eventually, of course, he did. Unfortunately, he taught his apprentice everything he knew. Then his apprentice killed him in his sleep. It's ironic. He could save others from death, but not himself."

Anakin asked, carefully, knowing how dangerous a question it was, "Is it possible to learn this power?"

Palpatine turned and looked him in the eye. "Not from a Jedi."

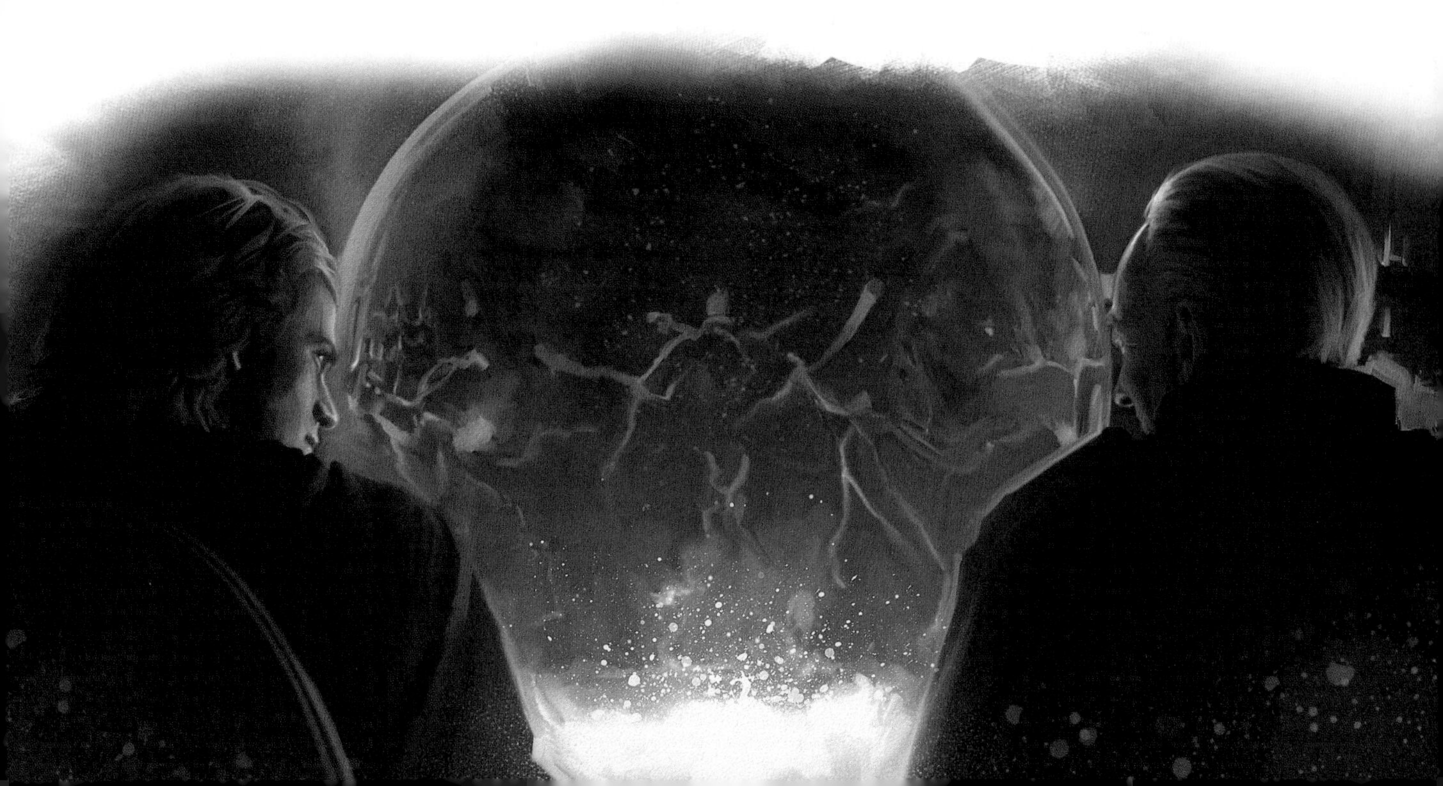

Anakin had hoped to be chosen by the Jedi Council to hunt down General Grievous in the Utapau system, but Yoda recommended that they send a Jedi Master with more experience: Obi-Wan.

Yoda himself was stationed on the forest planet Kashyyyk to help the clone army and the native Wookiees fight off the Separatist droid army there. Many of the Jedi Masters were likewise doing their part, stationed all over the galaxy, but they voted via hologram in support of Obi-Wan.

Anakin was worried he had disappointed his master, but Obi-Wan clasped his shoulder. Despite his frustrations with the Jedi Order, and even with his friend and former teacher, Anakin cared for Obi-Wan.

"You are strong and wise, Anakin, and I am very proud of you. You have become a far greater Jedi than I could ever hope to be," Obi-Wan encouraged. "But you must be patient. It will not be long before the Council makes you a Jedi Master."

Bolstered and reassured, Anakin wished Obi-Wan well on his journey. "May the Force be with you!"

"Good-bye, old friend," Obi-Wan replied. "May the Force be with you."

But Anakin dreamed again that Padmé died during childbirth. This time, the vision included Obi-Wan urging Padmé not to give up. And yet the vision did not include Anakin himself.

"Obi-Wan's been here, hasn't he?" Anakin asked angrily as he sat in Padmé's apartment. Obi-Wan must have stopped by before he left for his mission.

"He came by this morning," Padmé replied, unconcerned. Obi-Wan may not have known the secret of her marriage to Anakin, but he was still a trusted friend to them both.

"He's worried about you," she told him. "He says you've been under a lot of stress."

"I feel lost," Anakin confessed. "Obi-Wan and the Council don't trust me. Something's happening. I'm not the Jedi I should be. I want more. And I know I shouldn't."

Padmé went to his side, her round belly sloping gently under her indigo gown. "You expect too much of yourself."

He turned to hold her, to reassure her. "I found a way to save you. From my nightmares. I won't lose you, Padmé."

She put both of her hands against his chest, smoothing down his Jedi robes. "I'm not going to die in childbirth, Ani. I promise you."

Anakin gazed into her eyes.

"No," he told her firmly. "I promise *you*."

When Obi-Wan arrived on the planet Utapau to hunt for General Grievous, the Pau'ans who greeted him informed him that Grievous was indeed on their planet—and that they were being held hostage.

"They are watching us," a Pau'an named Tion Medon whispered to Obi-Wan. "Tenth level. Thousands of battle droids."

"Tell your people to take shelter," the Jedi advised.

Obi-Wan sent his ship back into space with a message for the Jedi Council and a plan for the clone troopers—and to make Grievous think the Jedi had left Utapau. Obi-Wan pulled the hood of his robe over his head and slunk back into the shadows of the cave-like structure where Grievous was hiding, remaining on the planet in secret.

The Jedi mounted a vibrant green varactyl named Boga and rode the reptilian steed up above the tenth level, where Tion Medon had said he would find General Grievous and his allies.

After overhearing Grievous tell the Trade Federation viceroy to travel to a planet called Mustafar, Obi-Wan leapt down to finish the cyborg warlord once and for all.

"Back away," Grievous told his droids. "I will deal with this Jedi slime myself."

"Your move," Obi-Wan said.

Grievous unbuckled his cloak. "You fool! I was trained in your Jedi arts by Count Dooku." When his arms were revealed, they split in two. Grievous now had four arms, and each hand held a lightsaber, claimed from past duels he had won!

Obi-Wan smiled, and the battle began. The Jedi managed to slice off two of the cyborg's hands, but Grievous was proving a difficult foe.

Fortunately, on cue, a battalion from the clone army arrived to help Obi-Wan.

"Army or not, you must realize you are doomed," Grievous spat.

"Oh, I don't think so," Obi-Wan replied.

He used the Force to throw Grievous into a girder, but the cyborg landed like a bug, scuttling away on six legs, and took off on a wheel bike.

Obi-Wan whistled for his varactyl and gave chase into the rocky sinkholes of Utapau.

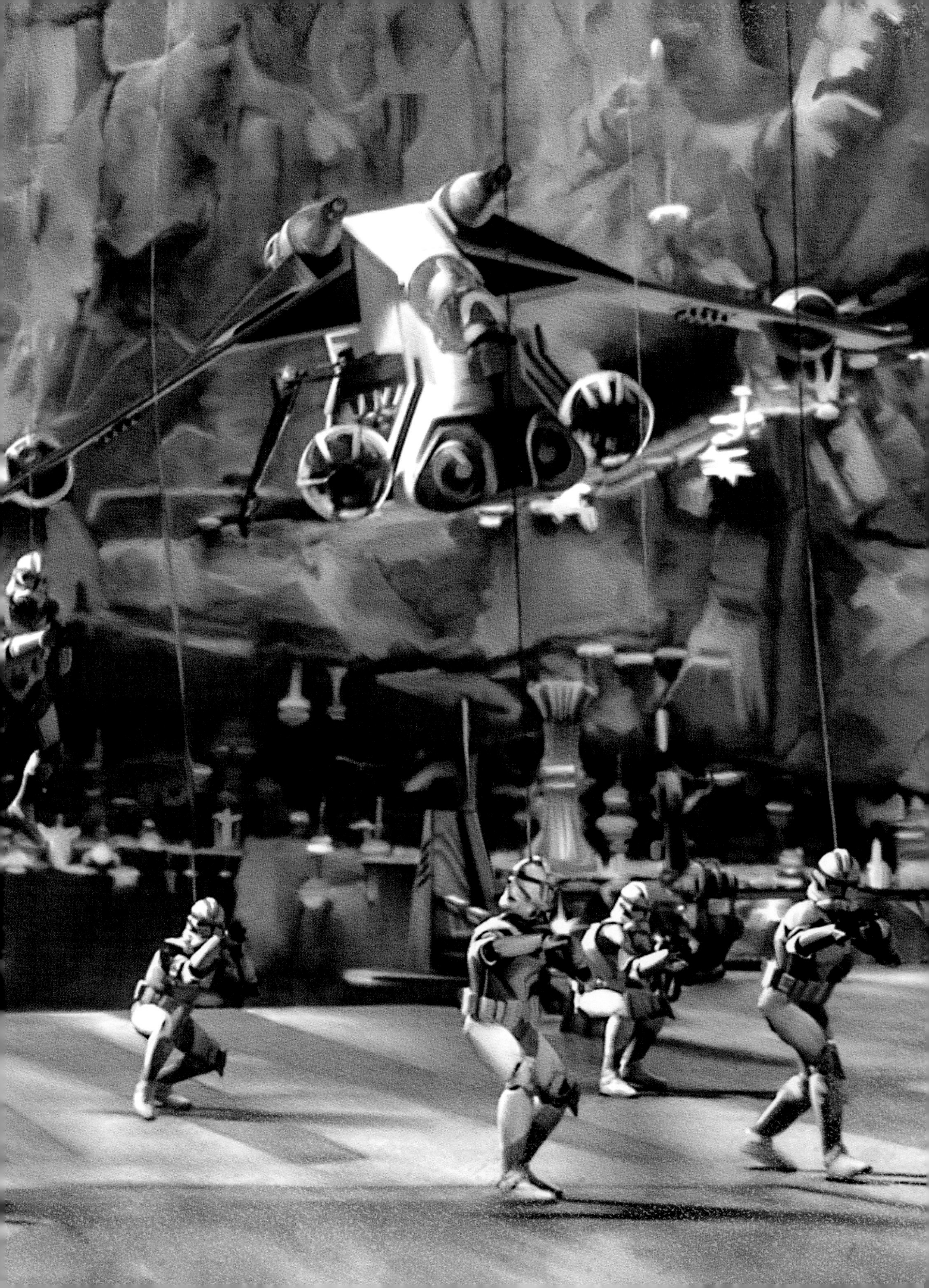

Back on Coruscant, the Jedi Council received a message from the clone army saying that Obi-Wan was in pursuit of Grievous on Utapau, and sent Anakin to tell Chancellor Palpatine.

Palpatine was disappointed that the Jedi Council had not sent Anakin to Utapau instead. He agreed that they did not seem to appreciate Anakin's talents.

"More and more, I get the feeling that I'm being excluded from the Jedi Council," Anakin told him. "I know there are things about the Force that they're not telling me."

"They don't trust you, Anakin," Palpatine said, which made Anakin burn with pride and anger. "They see your future. They know your power will be too strong to control. You must break through the fog of lies the Jedi have created around you. Let me help you to know the subtleties of the Force."

That caught Anakin by surprise.

"How do you know the ways of the Force?"

"My mentor taught me everything about the Force. Even the nature of the dark side."

Anakin looked at him sharply. "You know the dark side?"

"Anakin, if one is to understand the great mystery, one must study all its aspects, not just the dogmatic, narrow view of the Jedi," Palpatine urged. "If you wish to become a complete and wise leader, you must embrace . . . a larger view of the Force."

Palpatine and Anakin began to circle each other, and Anakin felt his fingers twitch toward his lightsaber. The things Palpatine was saying . . . they were dangerous.

“Be careful of the Jedi, Anakin. Only through me can you achieve a power greater than any Jedi. Learn to know the dark side of the Force, and you will be able to save your wife from certain death.”

Excitement battled the tension in Anakin’s heart.

“What did you say?”

Palpatine stopped and faced him. “Use my knowledge, I beg you.”

But Anakin was a Jedi, and he knew that what Palpatine offered him was wrong. He stepped away, igniting his lightsaber to block the Chancellor’s path as all the pieces came together in his mind: Palpatine was a Sith Lord!

But Palpatine showed no fear at Anakin’s understanding. He didn’t tremble or apologize. He merely went back to circling warily.

“I know what’s been troubling you. Don’t continue to be a pawn of the Jedi Council. Ever since I’ve known you, you’ve been searching for a life greater than an ordinary Jedi.” Palpatine turned his back. “Are you going to kill me?”

“I would certainly like to,” Anakin replied, recognizing the evil that could only come from a Sith Lord.

“I know you would,” Palpatine whispered. “I can feel your anger. It gives you focus. Makes you stronger.” He turned back, but Anakin holstered his saber.

“I’m going to turn you over to the Jedi Council,” he said. Anakin knew it was the right thing to do.

“Of course. You should.” Palpatine faced him, unafraid and unashamed. “But you’re not sure of their intentions, are you? You have great wisdom, Anakin. Know the power of the dark side. The power to save Padmé.”

Anakin went directly to Mace Windu, who was eager to tell him that they had heard word that Obi-Wan had defeated Grievous. It was time for Chancellor Palpatine to end the war and return all power to the democracy of the Senate.

"He won't give up his power," Anakin said, informing Mace of what he had discovered about Palpatine.

Mace was horrified to learn the truth about the Chancellor, but he knew they needed to act quickly. Anakin asked to go with the Jedi to confront Palpatine, but the older Jedi insisted that Anakin stay behind.

"I sense a great deal of confusion in you, young Skywalker. There is much fear that clouds your judgment. Wait in the Council Chambers until we return."

As Anakin waited in the chamber at sunset, he was haunted by Palpatine's words. If the Jedi destroyed him, any chance of saving Padmé would be lost. . . .

Anakin hurried to Palpatine's chambers. There, he found a frightened Palpatine cowering against a broken window as Jedi Master Mace Windu loomed over him, his violet lightsaber ready to strike.

"You are under arrest, my lord," Mace said.

"Anakin, I told you it would come to this," Palpatine whimpered. "I was right. The Jedi are taking over."

"The oppression of the Sith will never return," Mace clarified. "You have lost."

But instead of surrendering, Palpatine shook his head. "No," he growled in a monstrous voice Anakin had never heard before. "No. You will die!"

Stretching out his gnarled fingers, Palpatine shot a violent burst of Force lightning at Mace Windu. Mace caught the lightning with his saber and shot it back at Palpatine, shouting to Anakin for help.

The two masters, one Jedi and one Sith, were caught in a vicious circle of lightning, and Anakin didn't know what to do.

"I have the power to save the one you love!" Palpatine howled as the lightning twisted his features and burned his skin. "You must choose!"

"Don't listen to him, Anakin," Mace said, his teeth gritted against the electricity.

But Palpatine was dying, his skin melting like wax. "Don't let him kill me," he begged. "I can't hold it any longer. I . . . I can't. I'm too weak. Anakin, help me." The lightning faded, and Palpatine fell back, barely alive.

"I am going to end this once and for all," Mace said, untouched by the lightning's power.

"You can't. He must stand trial," Anakin reminded him.

Still, Mace did not back down. "He has control of the Senate and the courts. He's too dangerous to be left alive."

"It's not the Jedi way," Anakin argued. "He must live."

But Anakin's reminders of the Jedi code and Palpatine's pleas did not stop Mace. He ignited his lightsaber and reared back to deliver a killing stroke.

Anakin watched the violet saber slash down and knew what he had to do. He drew his own lightsaber and slashed off Mace's hand at the wrist. Palpatine's twisted face lit up with victory.

"Power!" he cried, aiming his lightning at Mace, who could no longer absorb the jolt with his lightsaber. "Unlimited power!"

Anakin watched in horror as blue electricity enrobed Master Windu and hurled him out the window to his death.

"What have I done?" Anakin asked weakly. His legs gave out beneath him, and he sat, letting his lightsaber tumble to the floor as he finally understood what he had allowed to happen.

"You're fulfilling your destiny, Anakin." Palpatine stood, no longer a weak old man. His face was twisted and destroyed, his eyes gone a sick yellow, but somehow he was more powerful than before.

"Become my apprentice. Learn to use the dark side of the Force."

Anakin looked up, fighting for breath.

"I will do whatever you ask," he said, knowing it was too late to turn back. "Just help me save Padmé's life. I can't live without her."

Palpatine's voice was deep, as if it rose from the very ground around Anakin. "To cheat death is a power only one has achieved, but if we work together, I know we can discover the secret."

Kneeling before the Sith, Anakin said, "I pledge myself to your teachings."

"Good. Good," his new master said. "The Force is strong with you. A powerful Sith you will become. Henceforth, you shall be known as Darth . . . Vader."

Palpatine told his new apprentice that when the Jedi learned what had happened, they would kill the Sith master and apprentice, along with all the senators — including Padmé.

"Every single Jedi, including your friend Obi-Wan Kenobi, is now an enemy of the Republic. We must move quickly. The Jedi are relentless. If they are not all destroyed, it will be civil war without end."

His new apprentice agreed. For he saw the truth of it: the Jedi had lost their way, and the Senate was indeed corrupt.

"First, I want you to go to the Jedi Temple," Palpatine told him. "Do what must be done. Do not hesitate. Show no mercy. Only then will you be strong enough with the dark side to save Padmé."

"What about the other Jedi spread throughout the galaxy?"

"Their betrayal will be dealt with," Palpatine said. "After you have finished your business at the Jedi Temple, go to the Mustafar system. Wipe out the Separatist leaders. Once more, the Sith will rule the galaxy. And we shall have peace."

Palpatine's smile was a frightening, skeletal thing, but the young man who had once been known as Anakin knew he must please his new master or else he'd never be able to save Padmé.

He marched into the Jedi Temple, leading a battalion of clones to destroy all those he found within and everything the Jedi held dear, thereby proving his devotion to the dark side — and his new master.

Meanwhile, Chancellor Palpatine — acting as Darth Sidious — contacted the clone army spread throughout the galaxy in the fight against the Separatist droid soldiers.

"The time has come," he told them. "Execute Order 66."

As one, just as they had been programmed to do, the clones turned on their Jedi companions. Jedi Knights of all species were taken by surprise — suddenly battling those who had fought alongside them not a moment before. In seconds, the powerful protectors of the galaxy were defeated, one by one.

On Kashyyyk, faithful Wookiees stepped in to protect Master Yoda from the clones who had turned on him. Two Wookiees known as Tarfful and Chewbacca led the small alien through the chaos to an escape pod in the mountains. Yoda needed to return to Coruscant—as did Obi-Wan, who had barely escaped from Utapau with his life.

Obi-Wan and Yoda snuck into the Jedi Temple. They needed to send an alert to any Jedi remaining in the galaxy, commanding them to go into hiding. The two Jedi were shocked by what they found there. The destruction was almost too much to bear.

But Yoda and Obi-Wan battled their way through the temple, defeating clones to send their most desperate message. Once they had finished the task at hand, Obi-Wan logged in to the security system to see who had wreaked such horror on the temple.

When he saw the holofootage of his friend and Padawan, Obi-Wan's heart nearly stopped beating. How could it be?

Padmé was relieved to see her husband when he finally returned to her apartment.

"Are you all right?" she asked him, checking him all over for battle wounds. "I heard there was an attack on the Jedi Temple."

"I'm fine," he assured her. "I came to see if you and the baby are safe."

He then told her that the Jedi had tried to overthrow the Republic. "I saw Master Windu attempt to assassinate the Chancellor myself."

But when she asked him what he was going to do, he turned away, unable to meet her eyes. "I will not betray the Republic. My loyalties lie with the Chancellor. And with the Senate. And with you."

"What about Obi-Wan?"

"I don't know. Many Jedi have been killed. We can only hope he's remained loyal to the Chancellor."

Padmé pressed against him, crying. "I'm afraid."

"Have faith, my love." He tenderly caressed her face. "The Chancellor has given me a very important mission. I'm going to Mustafar to end this war. Wait for me until I return. Things will be different, I promise."

The new Sith apprentice landed on the lava-covered planet Mustafar and strode into the Separatist command room with his hood cloaking his face.

"Welcome, Lord Vader," the Trade Federation viceroy said. "We've been expecting you."

Without a word, Anakin used the Force to seal the room and destroy the Separatist leaders who'd driven the war with their greed. They didn't know they'd been pawns of the Sith all along, and their usefulness had reached an end.

Back on Coruscant, Chancellor Palpatine told the Galactic Senate that the Jedi were to be hunted down after they'd attempted to assassinate him. Granted even more powers by the government, he stated that the Galactic Republic would become the Galactic Empire, of which he would be emperor.

The Senate hall erupted in cheers, the delegates under the spell of the Emperor's power and his promises of safety, protection, and peace.

"So this is how liberty dies," Padmé said from her place in the stands. "With thunderous applause."

When Obi-Wan came to tell Padmé what had become of Anakin, Padmé refused to believe that the man she loved was capable of turning to the dark side. Obi-Wan needed to find Anakin, but Padmé wouldn't tell Obi-Wan where he was, for she knew that Obi-Wan would have no choice but to kill his former apprentice.

Padmé believed she could still save her husband. She was the only one who knew his deepest self. She could turn him away from the dark side. Taking only C-3PO with her, she flew to Mustafar, unaware that Obi-Wan had hidden in her ship.

The Sith apprentice recognized Padmé's chrome-plated ship as it docked on Mustafar and ran out to meet her. Padmé hurried down the ramp to embrace him.

"I was so worried about you," she said. "Obi-Wan told me terrible things."

Furious with his old master once more, the new Sith apprentice seethed.

"Obi-Wan is trying to turn you against me."

"No. He cares about us. He knows about us. Anakin, all I want is your love!"

But Anakin was no more. Darth Vader had taken over.

"Love won't save you, Padmé. Only my new powers can do that."

"At what cost? You're a good person. Don't do this," she begged him, red lava reflected in her shining eyes.

"I am becoming more powerful than any Jedi has ever dreamed of. And I'm doing it for you. To protect you."

But she resisted. "Come with me. Help me raise our child. Leave everything else behind while we still can."

"Don't you see?" he asked her. "We don't have to run away anymore. I have brought peace to the Republic. I am more powerful than the Chancellor. I can overthrow him. And together, you and I can rule the galaxy, make things the way we want them to be!"

But instead of joining him, instead of embracing him and thanking him, the woman he loved backed away, shaking her head. "I don't believe what I'm hearing. Obi-Wan was right. You've changed."

Hearing his former master's name again, he grew angry with her. "I don't want to hear anything more about Obi-Wan. The Jedi turned against me. Don't you turn against me!"

Padmé was crying, still backing away. "Anakin, you're breaking my heart. You're going down a path I can't follow."

"Because of Obi-Wan."

"Because of what you've done! What you plan to do. Stop now. Come back. I love you."

But he wasn't looking at her anymore, wasn't listening to her pleading.

His rival, Obi-Wan Kenobi, had appeared on the ramp of Padmé's ship. She'd brought him there. Which meant everything she'd just said was a lie.

"You're with him! You brought him here to kill me!" Lifting his hand, Darth Vader used the Force to choke Padmé, to silence her, to punish her for hurting him so. Everything he'd done, he'd done for her, and she'd betrayed him!

"Anakin!" she gasped, her hands at her throat.

"Let her go!" Obi-Wan commanded.

And he did. Not because Obi-Wan told him to, but because he needed to focus on his true enemy: his old master. Looking down at Padmé, Vader felt a rush of shame and rage, which he focused on Obi-Wan.

"You turned her against me!" he shouted.

But Obi-Wan remained frustratingly calm. "You have done that yourself."

Darth Vader paced around the landing pad, the warm winds off the lava pits burning his scarred face. "You will not take her from me!"

"Your anger and your need for power have already done that." Obi-Wan threw off his brown Jedi robes and began to pace, as well, circling with his former apprentice. "You have allowed this dark lord to twist your mind. You have become the very thing you swore to destroy."

"Don't lecture me, Obi-Wan. I see through the lies of the Jedi. I do not fear the dark side, as you do. I have brought peace, freedom, justice, and security to my new empire."

"Your new empire?" Obi-Wan asked disbelievingly.

The Sith turned, unable to look at the man he had once loved as a brother. "Don't make me kill you."

"Anakin, my allegiance is to the Republic, to democracy!"

"If you're not with me . . ." Vader glared over his shoulder, "then you're my enemy!"

"Only a Sith deals in absolutes." Obi-Wan unhooked his lightsaber and got into a fighting stance. "I will do what I must."

"You will try," Vader replied as they both ignited their lightsabers.

Vader flipped toward Obi-Wan, and the duel began.

They battled their way through the war rooms of the base on Mustafar and outside across machinery that laced over the deadly flowing lava.

Obi-Wan knew his former apprentice's every move, and Vader knew the Jedi Master's ways, as well. Their blue sabers flashed as Jedi and Sith each sought the winning stroke.

Meanwhile, on Coruscant, Yoda hobbled into Emperor Palpatine's chambers.

"I hear a new apprentice you have, Emperor. Or should I call you . . . Darth Sidious?"

"Master Yoda. You survived," Palpatine hissed. "Now you will experience the full power of the dark side." Lashing out with his Force lightning, Palpatine threw Yoda to the ground. "I have waited a long time for this moment, my little green friend. At last, the Jedi are no more."

As the Emperor cackled, Yoda stood.

"Not if anything to say about it, I have. If so powerful you are, why leave?"

"You will not stop me. Darth Vader will become more powerful than either of us."

"Faith in your apprentice, misplaced may be," Yoda warned him. "As is your faith in the dark side of the Force."

The two grand foes began to fight, first throwing senatorial pods at each other, then turning to Force lightning. Yoda was thrown to the ground as the Emperor scrambled upward. Using his small size to his advantage, Yoda clambered into a vent, alerting his friend and ally Senator Bail Organa to his need for rescue. His prey lost, Emperor Palpatine called his ship. He sensed his apprentice was in danger.

"Into exile I must go," Yoda told Bail. "Failed, I have."

Back on Mustafar, Vader and Obi-Wan took to brawling with hands and fists — this fight was personal. They were evenly matched, and as each man recovered his saber, the battle grew more intense. They attempted to Force throw each other at the same time, and the resulting power tossed each man back. The fight moved to an outdoor balcony, Mustafar's lava fields lighting the scene a grisly red. Their duel took them onto a narrow pipe over the lava, and then Obi-Wan was forced to jump down to a catwalk even closer to the blistering hot lava. The structure on which they fought collapsed, and both men fought for purchase as they hurtled toward a waterfall of fire. Swinging from wires, they clashed in the sky, and then Obi-Wan dropped to a floating dock of metal barely skimming over the surface of the river of lava.

Vader only survived the drop thanks to his new Force powers, which he used to leap onto a lava-skimming droid. Directing the droid toward Obi-Wan's refuge, he started up the duel again.

"I have failed you, Anakin," Obi-Wan said.

"I should've known the Jedi were plotting to take over."

"Anakin, the Chancellor is evil!"

"From my point of view, the Jedi are evil!" Vader shot back.

"Well then, you are lost."

They floated above the lava, lightsabers lit. Each man hoped to turn his friend's heart to his own side.

Each man was disappointed.

"This is the end for you, my master," Vader said. He flipped onto Obi-Wan's platform, and their lightsabers clashed.

As they drifted near the blackened shore, Obi-Wan leapt to safety, calling down, "It's over, Anakin. I have the high ground."

"You underestimate my power," Vader told him.

"Don't try it!" Obi-Wan warned.

But Obi-Wan was no longer his master, and Vader did as he pleased. Summoning the Force, he leapt high in the air, slashing down at Obi-Wan.

With one stroke of his saber, Obi-Wan sliced off both of Vader's legs and his left arm. The Sith's world exploded in pain, but he wasn't going to give up. He landed on the hot coals of the shore, his lightsaber lost, and crawled toward Obi-Wan with hate in his heart.

Obi-Wan stood impossibly far away. "You were the chosen one! It was said that you would destroy the Sith, not join them – bring balance to the Force, not leave it in darkness." He picked up the lightsaber he had helped his once apprentice craft.

"I hate you!" Vader screamed, still crawling.

"You were my brother, Anakin. I loved you."

As if incited by Obi-Wan's words, fire erupted across Vader's body, wreathing him in flame. Yet still he crawled toward Obi-Wan, who simply walked away.

Hate was the only thing keeping Vader alive now.

When he first saw his true master's black robes approaching him on Mustafar, Vader thought he was dreaming. After being placed on a hovergurney and floated onto Palpatine's ship, the young Sith underwent surgery on Coruscant and was given prosthetic limbs to replace the legs and arm he'd lost. He felt every prick of a needle, every centimeter of burned flesh. His world had become nothing but pain and hate. But still, under all that hurt, he longed for Padmé.

On Mustafar, Obi-Wan returned to Padmé's ship. She was weak, barely conscious, but still she roused to ask, "Is Anakin all right?"

Fortunately, she fell back asleep before he was forced to answer. Obi-Wan knew she was in trouble, so he piloted her ship away from the wretched lava planet to the secret base where Yoda hid with Bail Organa on an asteroid called Polis Massa.

"Medically, she's completely healthy. For reasons we can't explain, we are losing her," a medical droid told Obi-Wan as Padmé lay unconscious in an operating suite.

"She's dying?" Obi-Wan asked, incredulous.

"She's lost the will to live. We need to operate quickly if we are to save the babies. She's carrying twins."

Padmé was awake as her babies were born. When the med droid showed her the first baby, a son, she touched his tiny face. "Oh, Luke," she said softly, naming him. The second baby, a girl, she named Leia. But her energy was giving out.

"Obi-Wan," she said, gasping, "there's good in him. I know there's . . . still . . ."

Having seen her children into the world, her heart too broken to continue, Padmé died.

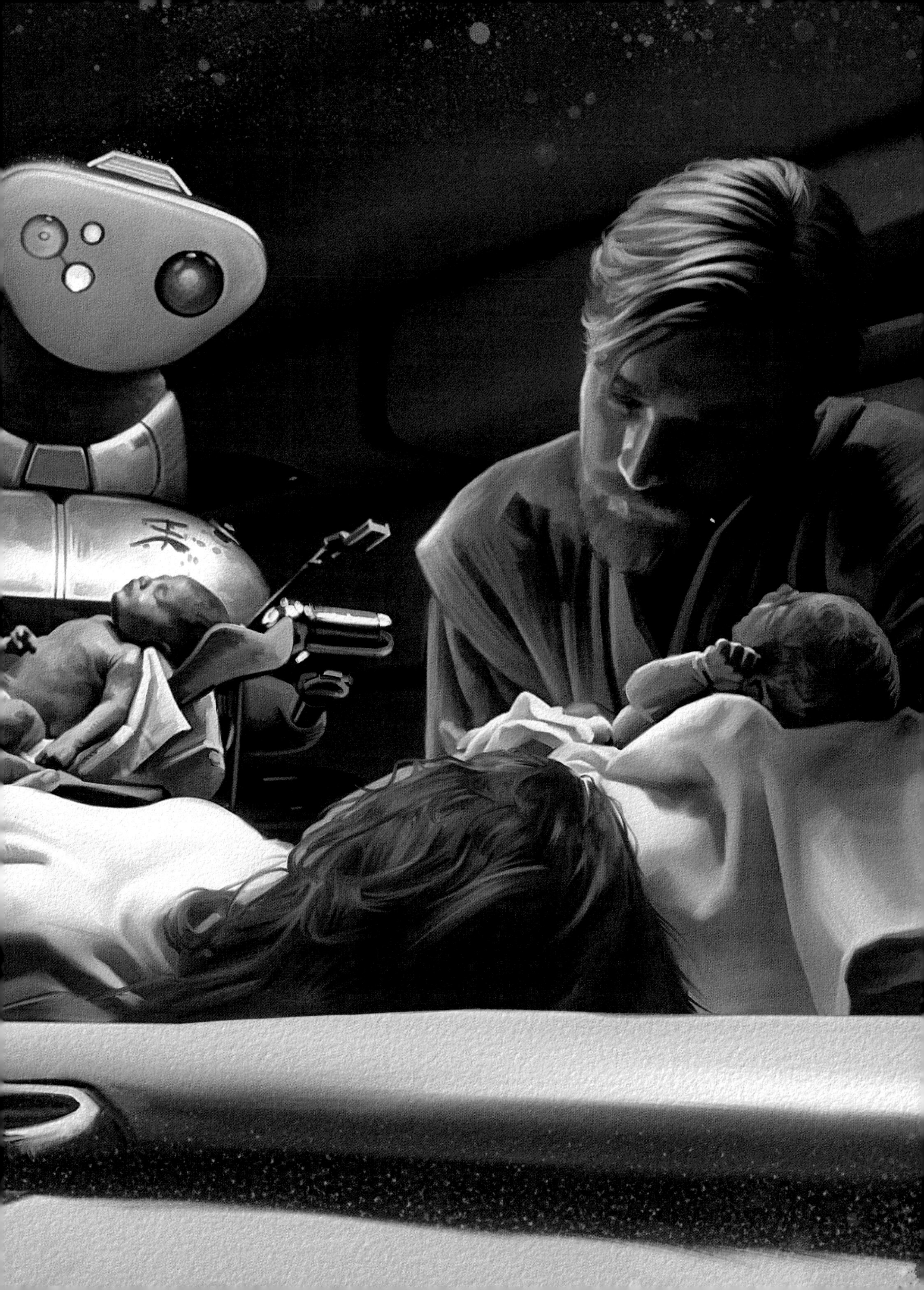

Vader stared into the blinding light of his own operating room as a shining black mask was placed over his face, helping him breathe through his smoke-damaged lungs. His entire body was encased in matching black armor, and the operating table tilted to help him stand.

"Lord Vader, can you hear me?" Emperor Palpatine asked.

"Yes, Master." Vader's voice was different, filtered through his mask and amplified. It was foreign to his own ears. "Where is Padmé? Is she safe? Is she all right?"

The Emperor gave him a pitying look. "It seems, in your anger, you killed her."

"I couldn't have. She was alive. I felt it!"

The Force coursed through the young Sith, filling him with cascades of anger and regret. He broke his bonds and stepped onto his new legs for the first time, screaming, "Nooooo!"

With both parents lost, Yoda and Obi-Wan decided that the twin babies must be split up for protection. Emperor Palpatine could never discover the truth of Anakin's children, who would surely grow up to be in tune with the Force.

A kind senator and friend of Padmé's, Bail Organa, took baby Leia to his wife on the planet Alderaan, where she would be raised as their beloved daughter and a princess.

Obi-Wan took Luke to Tatooine, where he entrusted the baby to Anakin's stepbrother, Owen Lars, and his wife, Beru. Obi-Wan would live nearby and secretly keep watch over his old friend's son.

"Until the time is right, disappear we will," Yoda told his allies with grim finality.

They were the only people in the galaxy who knew that the children of the Jedi's chosen one lived. Even C-3PO's databanks were wiped, although R2 kept his memories.

Anakin Skywalker, once fabled to bring balance to the Force, had become Darth Vader and a dark lord of the Sith. He had no idea that before she died of a broken heart, his beloved wife, Padmé, had given birth to not one but two children.

Palpatine's Empire ruled. But perhaps one day the galaxy would again know peace.

With Leia and Luke, a new hope was born.

A NEW HOPE

In a distant galaxy, a civil war raged as an evil empire ruled with an iron grip. No planet seemed beyond its grasp; no star system could escape its clutches. From the parched landscapes of Jakku to the bustling city planet Coruscant, all fell under cruel Emperor Palpatine's reign. For Palpatine was the shadowy Sith Lord Darth Sidious, and together with his powerful apprentice, Darth Vader, it seemed as though nothing would be left untouched by the dark side of the Force.

And yet a spark of hope dared to burn in the face of such overwhelming odds. A tenacious group called the Rebel Alliance rose to fight the Empire's control and managed to steal the plans for its most powerful weapon, the dreaded Death Star.

Few people lived to tell of the Empire's darker dealings, and to some, the rebels were merely a nuisance. Stormtroopers roamed the streets, and the Jedi—wielders of the light side of the Force who had once fought for peace and justice throughout the galaxy—had become all but a myth, leaving the Force badly out of balance.

But that balance began to shift when a young farm boy on the forgotten desert planet Tatooine felt a call to adventure. . . .

Luke Skywalker had lived on Tatooine all his life. He had grown up on his uncle Owen's moisture farm, using complex equipment to siphon water from the harsh deserts. It was a boring life, and Skywalker, a young man of nineteen, longed for adventure.

Luke hoped to apply to the Imperial Academy and see more of the galaxy, but his uncle Owen and aunt Beru needed his help on the farm. Thus, the boy remained tethered in place, toiling among the sand dunes. But one day, something curious happened after he and his uncle bought two droids from some passing Jawa traders.

One was a golden protocol droid called C-3PO, and the other was an astromech droid called R2-D2.

While Luke was cleaning R2, the little droid suddenly played part of a hologram message from a young woman dressed in white robes.

"Help me, Obi-Wan Kenobi," she said urgently. "You're my only hope."

Luke was intrigued by the message. The young woman was clearly in distress. But when he asked to see the entire message, R2 beeped stubbornly.

"He says he's the property of Obi-Wan Kenobi, a resident of these parts," C-3PO translated. "It's a private message for him."

"Obi-Wan Kenobi," Luke mused. "I wonder if he means old Ben Kenobi."

Later, at dinner, Luke told his uncle Owen about the message and asked him about Ben Kenobi, a hermit who lived out beyond the Dune Sea. Uncle Owen brushed Luke's curiosity aside, saying Kenobi had died about the same time as Luke's father.

"He knew my father?" Luke's curiosity only grew. He didn't know much about either of his parents.

"I told you to forget it," Uncle Owen replied, ending the conversation.

But that night, Luke discovered that R2-D2 had rolled off into the dangerous dunes to deliver his message. The droid was important, and Luke had to find him. It seemed as though Luke was bound for adventure, whether his uncle liked it or not.

The next morning, Luke hopped in his landspeeder with C-3PO and followed R2's trail across the desert. Fortunately, they soon found the missing droid in a distant, craggy ravine. Unfortunately, ferocious Tusken Raiders quickly leapt from behind the rocks, braying angrily as one of them knocked Luke unconscious with a gaderffii stick.

When Luke woke up, a robed form kneeled over him.

"Rest easy, son. You've had a busy day," an old man with a white beard said. "You're fortunate to be all in one piece."

Luke rubbed his head and focused his eyes. He couldn't believe who it was.

"Ben Kenobi? Boy, am I glad to see you!"

The old man seemed unsurprised. "Tell me, young Luke, what brings you out this far?"

Pointing at R2, Luke said, "This little droid. He's searching for his former master. He claims to be the property of Obi-Wan Kenobi. Is he a relative of yours?"

Old Ben sat down heavily, looking shaken. "Obi-Wan Kenobi? Now that's a name I've not heard in a long time."

"I think my uncle knows him. He said he was dead."

"Oh, he's not dead. Not yet." Ben smiled. "He's me."

Hearing that, R2 beeped excitedly.

"I haven't gone by the name of Obi-Wan since before you were born."

Hearing the call of more Tusken Raiders, Luke, Obi-Wan, and R2-D2 gathered up a battered C-3PO and sought refuge in Obi-Wan's home nearby.

As Luke fixed C-3PO, he had many questions for the old man, who went by Ben and said he had known Luke's father but seemed to misremember some of the details. "No, my father didn't fight in the Clone Wars," Luke told him. "He was a navigator on a spice freighter."

"That's what your uncle told you," Obi-Wan said with a grin. "He didn't hold with your father's ideals. Thought he ought to stay here and not get involved."

That got Luke's attention. "You fought in the Clone Wars?"

Ben smiled. "Yes, I was once a Jedi Knight, the same as your father."

Luke was overcome with emotion hearing that his father had been a great man and a mystical Jedi. "I wish I'd known him."

Obi-Wan, unlike Uncle Owen, seemed glad to talk about Luke's father. "He was the best star pilot in the galaxy and a cunning warrior. And he was a good friend. Which reminds me. I have something here for you. Your father wanted you to have this when you were old enough."

Obi-Wan rummaged in a trunk and presented Luke with a strange metal object. "It's your father's

lightsaber. This is the weapon of a Jedi Knight."

Luke thumbed a switch, and a bright blue blade of energy burst from the hilt. He waved the weapon back and forth, enjoying the blade's hum.

"An elegant weapon for a more civilized age," Obi-Wan said. "For over a thousand generations, the Jedi Knights were the guardians of peace and justice in the Old Republic. Before the dark times. Before the Empire."

Luke flicked off the saber's blade and sat down. "How did my father die?"

"A young Jedi named Darth Vader—who was a pupil of mine until he turned to evil—helped the Empire hunt down and destroy the Jedi Knights. He betrayed and murdered your father. Now the Jedi are all but extinct. Vader was seduced by the dark side of the Force."

"The Force?" Luke hadn't heard the term before, but he could tell it was important.

"The Force is what gives the Jedi power. It's an energy field created by all living things. It surrounds us and penetrates us. It binds the galaxy together."

Luke had heard of the Jedi, but he had thought those stories were just legends, tales of wizards and magic. No Jedi had been seen in decades. And yet what Obi-Wan had said, and the feel of his father's lightsaber in his hand, seemed true and somehow . . . right.

Then R2 played the young woman's full message for Obi-Wan.

She spoke formally and with great command: "General Kenobi, years ago you served my father in the Clone Wars. Now he begs you to help him in his struggle against the Empire. I regret that I am unable to present my father's request to you in person. But my ship has fallen under attack, and I'm afraid my mission to bring you to Alderaan has failed. I have placed information vital to the survival of the Rebellion into the memory systems of this R2 unit. My father will know how to retrieve it. You must see this droid safely delivered to him on Alderaan. This is our most desperate hour."

And then she said the words that had first sparked Luke's curiosity: "Help me, Obi-Wan Kenobi. You're my only hope."

Obi-Wan leaned forward, holding Luke in his gaze. "You must learn the ways of the Force if you're to come with me to Alderaan. I need your help, Luke. *She* needs your help."

Luke remembered all his responsibilities on the farm.

"I can't get involved. I've got work to do. It's not that I like the Empire — I hate it — but there's nothing I can do about that right now."

"Learn about the Force, Luke," Obi-Wan pressed again.

Luke *had* always dreamed of leaving Tatooine, but suddenly the galaxy felt too boundless, too uncertain.

"You must do what you feel is right, of course," Obi-Wan said, as if he could sense the war waging in the farm boy's heart.

Luke offered to take Obi-Wan to the nearest city so the old Jedi could get off-world and start his journey to Alderaan. But as they zoomed across the desert, they found a Jawa sandcrawler that had been destroyed by Imperial stormtroopers. It was the same group of Jawas that had sold the droids to Luke and his uncle. The old man and the boy realized that the Imperial troopers were after C-3PO and R2-D2 – no doubt due to the vital information R2 carried that the young woman had mentioned in her message.

Luke hurried home to warn his uncle Owen and aunt Beru, but he was too late. He found smoke rising from their ravaged home. Luke's aunt and uncle had been killed by the Empire.

"There's nothing you could've done, Luke," Obi-Wan assured him. "You would've been killed, too, and the droids would be in the hands of the Empire."

But for Luke, everything had changed. The Empire had always seemed far away – a terrible threat, to be sure, but one that was distant and impersonal. Now he had seen firsthand what it could do, and he understood why the galaxy needed the Rebellion. He also began to realize that perhaps he had his own part to play.

"I want to come with you," he told Obi-Wan. "There's nothing for me here now. I want to learn the ways of the Force and become a Jedi like my father."

Obi-Wan clasped Luke's shoulder warmly and nodded.

They took off in Luke's landspeeder and headed for Mos Eisley spaceport, where they would find a ship to take them to Alderaan.

"You will never find a more wretched hive of scum and villainy," Obi-Wan warned as they zoomed into town. "We must be cautious."

Indeed, they were soon stopped by a detachment of white-armored stormtroopers searching for any sign of the missing droids. Luke realized they were caught, and fear crawled up his spine.

"How long have you had these droids?" the lead trooper asked.

"Three or four seasons," Luke lied.

"They're up for sale, if you want them," Obi-Wan added.

"Let me see your identification."

But Obi-Wan waved his hand and told the trooper, "You don't need to see his identification."

"We don't need to see his identification," the trooper repeated.

"These aren't the droids you're looking for. He can go about his business. Move along," Obi-Wan continued.

"These aren't the droids we're looking for," the trooper said, waving them away. "He can go about his business. Move along."

When they were safely past and had parked the speeder, Luke turned to Obi-Wan. "I can't understand how we got by those troops. I thought we were dead!"

Obi-Wan pulled up his hood. "The Force can have a strong influence on the weak-minded."

As they neared an open door, Obi-Wan warned Luke that the cantina they were about to enter to find a pilot could be rough, but Luke thought he was ready for anything.

Luke was wrong. Ducking in the door, he found himself surrounded by more aliens than he'd ever seen. As a Bith band played a jaunty tune, the bartender pointed at C-3PO and R2-D2.

"Hey! We don't serve their kind here," the bartender shouted. "Your droids will have to wait outside."

Luke sent the droids back to the speeder, but he'd already attracted the wrong kind of attention. A tall Aqualish man with large black eyes and closely set tusks shoved Luke's shoulder with a vicious growl. Luke turned back to the bar, trying to avoid trouble. But then a second man poked his shoulder.

"He doesn't like you," the pig-nosed human said, pointing to his Aqualish friend.

"I'm sorry," Luke said, again looking away.

"I don't like you, either!" the man shouted, one hand crushing Luke's shoulder. "You just watch yourself. We're wanted men. I have the death sentence on twelve systems."

"I'll be careful," Luke promised him.

"You'll be *dead*!"

Obi-Wan intervened, telling the man, "This little one's not worth the effort. Let me buy you a drink."

Instead, the man threw Luke into a table and aimed his blaster at Obi-Wan. Luke watched from the floor in surprise as Obi-Wan calmly drew his lightsaber, deflected the two men's blaster bolts, and slashed off the Aqualish man's arm with his blade!

As if nothing had happened, the band started up again and the bar returned to its noisy hum.

Obi-Wan helped Luke up and introduced him to a tall, hairy Wookiee known as Chewbacca and a pilot named Han Solo. After a bit of haggling and boasting on Han's part, they reached an agreement for passage to Alderaan on Han's ship, the *Millennium Falcon*, and split up, agreeing to meet at docking bay 94.

"What a piece of junk!" Luke exclaimed when he arrived and saw Han's ship.

But Han knew better. "She may not look like much, but she's got it where it counts, kid. Now, we're a little rushed, so if you'll get on board, we'll get out of here."

Luke and Obi-Wan entered the ship, but before Han could take off, stormtroopers showed up, blasters firing. Han shot back at them, running up the *Falcon*'s ramp, and yelled, "Chewie, get us out of here!"

The *Millennium Falcon* took off, evading the guns of three Imperial battleships, and blasted into hyperspace.

They were on their way to Alderaan, and the journey had already proven to be unlike anything Luke had ever experienced.

As the *Falcon* sailed through space, Luke began his Jedi training. Obi-Wan instructed him to tune in to the Force and use his lightsaber to practice deflecting random electric blasts from a floating training remote.

But right in the midst of the lesson, Obi-Wan suddenly fell silent.

"What's wrong?" Luke asked him.

"I felt a great disturbance in the Force," Obi-Wan explained, clearly concerned. "As if millions of voices suddenly cried out in terror and were silenced. I fear something terrible has happened."

Then, shaking his head, Obi-Wan urged Luke to get back to his training. Han had joined them from the ship's cockpit, and he laughed when the training remote managed to zap Luke with a rogue blast.

"Hokey religions and ancient weapons are no match for a good blaster at your side, kid," he said.

Obi-Wan smiled and reached for a helmet.

"I suggest you try it again, Luke," the Jedi said, placing the helmet on the boy's head. "This time let go of your conscious self and act on instinct."

"But with the blast shield down, I can't even see," Luke protested.

"Your eyes can deceive you," Obi-Wan replied. "Don't trust them."

Luke drew a deep breath and did as he was told. He felt the Force flowing through him, guiding his movements, and soon he was able to deflect the oncoming zaps without seeing them.

"You see, you can do it," Obi-Wan encouraged. "You've taken your first step into a larger world."

The *Millennium Falcon* soon dropped out of hyperspace, but something was terribly wrong. Instead of seeing the planet Alderaan, they found only a new asteroid field!

"It's been blown away," Han said, surprised.

"Destroyed by the Empire," Obi-Wan agreed sadly. That was the disturbance in the Force he had felt earlier.

Suddenly, an Imperial TIE fighter screamed past them.

"It's headed for that small moon," Luke said, pointing at a round gray planet before them.

When Obi-Wan looked up, his eyes went wide. "That's no moon. It's a space station."

"I have a very bad feeling about this," Luke muttered.

Chewbacca groaned in agreement.

"Turn the ship around," Obi-Wan urged.

But it was too late. The *Falcon* was caught in the space station's powerful tractor beam.

"There's got to be something you can do," Luke said, looking at Han.

"Nothing I can do about it, kid," Han replied, powering down the ship as it was pulled into one of the space station's hangar bays. "But they're not going to get me without a fight."

"You can't win," Obi-Wan said. "But there *are* alternatives to fighting."

Obi-Wan was right. The group hid in secret compartments on board the *Falcon* to evade capture. When a couple of stormtroopers entered the seemingly empty ship for inspection, Han and Chewie took them out so that Han and Luke could put on the Imperial armor and infiltrate the bridge with Chewie and the droids. R2-D2 tapped into the space station's network while Obi-Wan took off alone to shut down the tractor beam so they could escape.

Luke wanted to go with Obi-Wan, but Obi-Wan told him to stay and protect the droids at all costs.

"Your destiny lies along a different path than mine," the old man said. "May the Force be with you, always."

Soon R2 beeped excitedly. C-3PO translated, letting everyone know that R2 had found the

young woman who had recorded the message. Her name was Princess Leia—and she was being held for execution in the very same space station!

"We have to do something!" Luke said. Already, he felt a connection to her.

"Don't get any funny ideas," Han said, putting his feet up on the console; he was just there for the money and was happy to stay put until Obi-Wan had turned off the tractor beam.

"But they're going to kill her!" Luke argued.

"Better her than me," Han shot back.

Han turned away, and Luke knew he had to think of some way to make the smuggler help him rescue Princess Leia.

He leaned over and whispered, "She's rich."

Han was suddenly willing to help, and Luke already had a plan.

Leaving the droids behind in the control room, Han and Luke posed as stormtroopers, with Chewie in binders as their prisoner. They marched him down to the detention block where the princess was being held. But once inside, they were challenged by Imperial guards and had to blast their way through.

Luke searched for the princess's cell. When he found her, his heart swelled with hope. To think that a strange message in a little droid had brought him all the way from Tatooine to an Imperial space station, where he was meeting an actual princess!

But Luke was still in his disguise, and the princess seemed unimpressed.

"Aren't you a little short for a stormtrooper?" she asked him.

Luke took off his helmet to show her that he was a friend. "I'm Luke Skywalker. I'm here to rescue you. I've got your R2 unit. I'm here with Ben Kenobi."

Leia was not one who typically needed rescuing, but when she heard Kenobi's name, she leapt to her feet.

"Ben Kenobi! Where is he?"

They dashed out of the cell and were met by Han and Chewie, who were firing blaster bolts down the cell bay. Stormtroopers were on their tail!

"Looks like you managed to cut off our only escape route," Leia observed.

"Maybe you'd like it back in your cell, Your Highness," Han barked.

As Han fought off the advancing troopers, Luke radioed C-3PO asking for help. But the droid told him there was no way out.

"I can't hold them off forever!" Han shouted.

Leia looked from Han to Luke. "This is some rescue! You came in here, but you didn't have a plan for getting out?"

Han continued to shoot at the stormtroopers, his face lit red by blaster fire. "He's the brains, sweetheart!"

"Well, I didn't—" Luke started, but Leia grabbed his blaster and shot open a nearby vent.

"Somebody has to save our skins," Leia growled. "Into the garbage chute, flyboy!"

Leia slipped down the chute, and Han urged Chewie to follow her.

"Wonderful girl!" Han yelled at Luke as they tried to pick off some of the troopers. "Either I'm going to kill her or I'm beginning to like her. Now get in there!"

Luke obeyed, diving down the chute with Han right behind him. It was a long slide down filthy pipes until Luke tumbled into a swampy mass of trash. Hoses, scrap metal, and food waste floated in smelly liquid. Han tried shooting the only door open, but his blaster bolt ricocheted dangerously from wall to wall.

"It's magnetically sealed!" Luke told him.

"It could be worse," Leia reminded them. As if in agreement, an unseen beast howled and clanked. Something lurked in the water below them!

Suddenly, Luke felt something wrap around his leg, and he was yanked underwater. He fought to stay afloat, but the creature soon had a meaty tentacle wrapped tightly around his neck. Trapped underwater, unable to breathe, Luke knew he couldn't survive. The farm boy from the desert world was going to die in a trash heap! But then, for what seemed like no reason at all, the creature let go of him. Luke scrambled for the surface and struggled to get to his feet, fighting for air.

Luke was free, but their problems were far from over.

The walls began to press inward.

They were in a trash compactor!

Han, Luke, Chewie, and Leia scrambled over the odd bits of debris to get to higher ground. They tried to brace the walls using a metal pipe, but the makeshift beam simply bent under the pressure.

Luke remembered the comlink he had brought with them from the bridge. He frantically tried contacting C-3PO and R2-D2 to have them disable the compactor through the computer terminal, but there was no reply. And all the while, the thick walls continued to move closer and closer together.

It seemed as if nothing could stop the heavy metal from crushing them.

At the last possible moment, C-3PO responded to Luke's call for help and R2 was able to shut down the garbage masher and open the door.

The droids had saved them!

As for Leia, she'd had enough of their so-called rescue.

"Listen, I don't know who you are or where you came from," she said to Han, "but from now on, you do as I tell you, okay?"

"Look, Your Worshipfulness," Han said, shooting an indignant look at Luke, "I take orders from one person: me."

"It's a wonder you're still alive," she replied.

"No reward is worth this!" Han moaned.

But Luke wasn't about to give up. They had to get back to their ship. Surely Obi-Wan had completed his mission to deactivate the tractor beam.

It wasn't long before they found the *Millennium Falcon.* Han distracted the stormtrooper guards while Luke and Leia ran for the hangar. Trapped by troopers on a ledge next to a chasm, Luke prepared to use a grappling line to swing to the other side.

"For luck," Leia said, kissing Luke on the cheek before they swung to safety.

Nearby, Obi-Wan crept through the corridors of the space station. He had indeed shut down the tractor beam, but he soon heard the ragged breathing of Darth Vader nearby.

Once a fellow Jedi and Obi-Wan's pupil and friend, Darth Vader had fallen to the dark side of the Force. They had battled once before, many years past, and now Vader stood before him again, red lightsaber glowing. Obi-Wan lit his own blue saber.

"I've been waiting for you, Obi-Wan," Vader said. "The circle is now complete. When I left you, I was but the learner. Now *I* am the master."

"Only a master of evil," Obi-Wan said, attacking with his saber.

They battled, red and blue blades flashing and humming.

"Your powers are weak, old man," Vader said.

"You can't win," Obi-Wan warned. "If you strike me down, I shall become more powerful than you can possibly imagine."

But Vader would not retreat. "You should not have come back."

Luke, Leia, Han, Chewie, and the droids had all reconvened in the hangar bay. They ran for the *Falcon*, but before Luke reached the ship, he heard the clash of lightsabers and turned to see his teacher engaged in a fierce duel.

"Ben!" he shouted, seeing Obi-Wan's saber crossed with Darth Vader's.

Ben looked to Luke, then looked back to Vader and smiled. He held up his blue lightsaber and closed his eyes. As Luke watched, helpless, Darth Vader struck the old man with a fatal blow!

And yet Obi-Wan didn't fall. His robes fluttered to the floor, empty, his lightsaber hilt landing neatly on top.

"No!" Luke shouted. He'd finally found a mentor, a man who knew the secrets of his father and could help him understand the Force. And now Obi-Wan was gone, leaving Luke alone in the galaxy—and unsure of his destiny.

The blaster fire from nearby stormtroopers roused Luke from his shock. He fought his way back to the ramp of the *Millennium Falcon*, firing at a nearby control panel to shut the blast doors before Vader could enter the hangar.

"Run, Luke. Run!" Obi-Wan's voice seemed to urge. It couldn't really be him, but Luke found comfort in it. And he took the advice.

Han and Chewie fired up the *Falcon* and blasted into space. With the tractor beam shut down, they were able to escape from the Death Star. But for Luke, it didn't feel like much of a victory. He slumped over the dejarik board in the *Falcon*'s lounge, feeling empty and lost. First Uncle Owen and Aunt Beru, and now Obi-Wan Kenobi. Leia placed a blanket over his shoulders.

"I can't believe he's gone," Luke told her.

"There wasn't anything you could've done," she gently assured him.

But then Han hurried past. "Come on, buddy. We're not out of this yet."

Even though Luke was distraught, he knew Han was right. Luke crawled down a ladder and into the *Falcon*'s lower gun turret, ready to do his part to fight off the Imperial TIEs that were zooming toward them. The ships came in fast, rocking the *Falcon* with laser blasts. Luke aimed again and again but kept missing, while Han had more experience and much better aim.

"I got him!" Luke cried when he finally took down a TIE.

"Don't get cocky, kid," Han warned him.

"There's still two more of them out there!" Leia reminded them.

Han and Luke each took down another fighter, and then Han engaged the hyperdrive.

"Not a bad bit of rescuing," he said, returning to his place in the cockpit as the blue lines of hyperspace streaked past. "Sometimes, I amaze even myself."

Leia raised an eyebrow. "That doesn't sound too hard. They let us go. That's the only explanation for the ease of our escape. They're tracking us."

Han shook his head. "Not this ship, sister!"

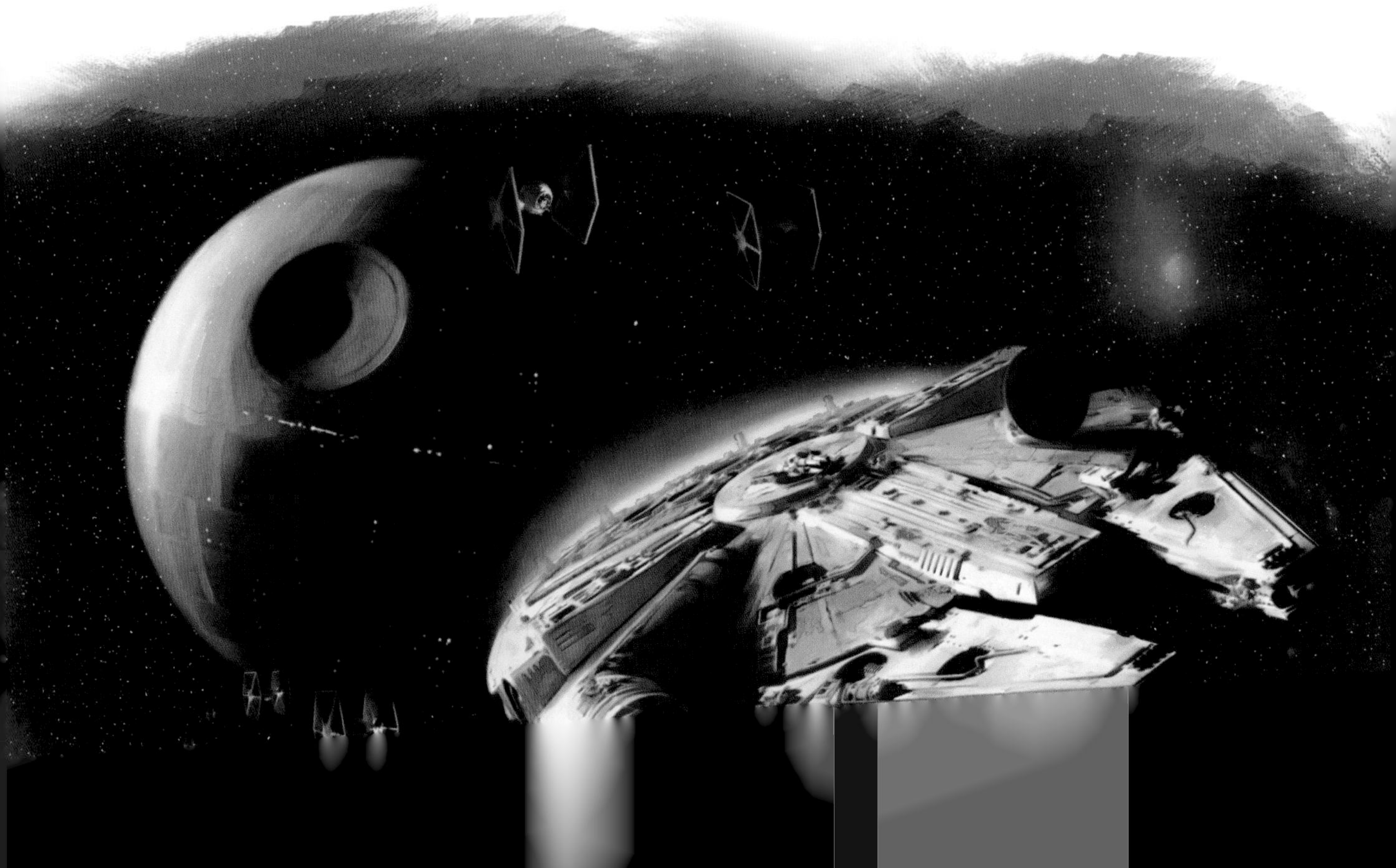

With a heavy sigh, Leia said, "At least the information in Artoo is still intact. He's carrying the technical readouts of that battle station. I only hope that when the data is analyzed a weakness can be found. It's not over yet."

"It is for me. Look, I ain't in this for your revolution, and I'm not in it for you, Princess. I expect to be well paid. I'm in it for the money."

Leia lifted her chin. "You needn't worry about your reward. If money is all that you love, then that's what you'll receive."

Giving him a sharp look, she squeezed past Luke and out of the cockpit, muttering, "Your friend is quite a mercenary. I wonder if he really cares about anything. Or anybody."

"I care!" Luke told her as she left. Then, turning to Han, he asked, "So, what do you think of her?"

Han rolled his eyes. "I'm trying not to, kid."

At that, Luke smiled and said, "Good."

Han reconsidered. "Still, she's got a lot of spirit. You think a princess like her and a guy like me could – "

"No!" Luke interrupted. He liked Leia, and Leia seemed to like him, but against a charming, seasoned pilot like Han . . . he had no chance.

Following Leia's coordinates, the *Falcon* soon landed at the secret rebel base on one of the moons of the planet Yavin. Luke was amazed to see the rebels he had heard so much about.

"Use the information in this R2 unit to plan the attack," Leia told the rebel commander. "It's our only hope."

Later, at a meeting, General Dodonna revealed to all the rebels, including Han and Luke, what they'd learned.

"The battle station is heavily shielded. Its defenses are designed around resisting a direct large-scale assault. A small, one-man fighter should be able to get past the outer defense. There's a weakness in the battle station. The approach will not be easy. You're required to maneuver straight down this trench and skim the surface to this point."

He pointed to a small square. "The target area is only two meters wide. It's a small thermal exhaust port. A precise hit will start a chain reaction, which should destroy the station. You'll have to use proton torpedoes."

One of the orange-clad pilots spoke up: "But that's impossible, even for a computer."

Luke leaned over to the pilot. "It's not impossible. I used to bull's-eye womp rats in my T-16 back home. They're not much bigger than two meters."

But the general ignored them both.

"Man your ships, and may the Force be with you," he told his pilots.

Impossible though it seemed, this was their only chance to shut down the Death Star before the Empire could use it to gain complete control over the galaxy.

The rebel pilots scrambled to their ships. Luke donned his own orange jumpsuit and joined them. He met Han on the way out.

"So you got your reward and you're just leaving?" Luke asked him, incredulous.

"That's right," Han said, loading cargo into the *Falcon*. "Say, why don't you come with us? You're pretty good in a fight. We could use you."

"Come on. Look around," Luke urged. "You know what's about to happen, what they're up against. They could use a good pilot like you. You're turning your back on them."

But Han just shook his head. "What good's a reward if you ain't around to use it? Attacking that battle station is suicide."

"Take care of yourself, Han. I guess that's what you're best at, isn't it?" Luke stormed away.

"Hey, Luke."

Luke turned around, hoping Han would make the right choice after all and join the rebel fight, but Han just said, "May the Force be with you."

Luke's eyes flicked accusingly to the containers holding Han's reward, and he jogged to his ship.

Leia wasn't as concerned about Han.

"He's got to choose his own path. No one can choose it for him," she told Luke.

"I only wish Ben were here," Luke replied.

Leia kissed him on the cheek and walked away. It helped knowing she was on his side, and as he hopped in his cockpit with R2 behind him, he finally felt as though he was exactly where he was supposed to be.

"Luke, the Force will be with you," Obi-Wan's voice said as Luke steered his X-wing into space with the other pilots.

As the rebel pilots all checked in on their way to the Death Star, Luke spoke into his helmet, naming his own position: "Red Five, standing by."

Suddenly, the sky was filled with fire. Turrets on the space station blasted the rebels with green turbolasers as TIE fighters swarmed out to mount a defense.

"Luke, trust your feelings."

Obi-Wan's voice in his head was so strong that Luke tapped his helmet, wondering if the comm was malfunctioning. But he had to concentrate on the battle. His fellow rebels were taking hits and crashing as they fought toward the trench that led to the crucial thermal exhaust port that could destroy the Death Star. Luke's ship took fire, and R2 worked to fix his shields as Luke waited his turn. He watched as Gold Team's Y-wings were targeted by Darth Vader's personal TIE fighter and crashed one by one in the trench.

But the explosions didn't scare Luke. Somehow, he knew that if he just had the chance to try, he could hit that port.

Finally, it was Luke's turn in the trench.

"Use the Force, Luke!" Obi-Wan's voice echoed in his mind. *"Let go, Luke."*

Luke felt the Force flow through him, felt Obi-Wan's presence, and followed his mentor's commands: he shut down his targeting computer and flew on instinct alone. Even with Vader and three other TIEs in pursuit, Luke trusted the Force to guide him onward.

What Luke didn't know was that the Death Star superlaser was aimed at the rebel base on Yavin 4. Leia was right: the Empire *had* tracked the *Falcon*. The Death Star was only moments away from reducing the moon, along with Princess Leia, to rubble. There wasn't much time.

With the computer off, Luke's X-wing jigged and juked, but finally Vader had it in his crosshairs, seconds from shooting Luke down. Suddenly, laser fire took down one of the TIE fighters, surprising Vader.

"Yahoo!" Han yelled through Luke's helmet comm as the *Millennium Falcon* swooped in. He took out the last two TIE fighters, sending Vader spinning into space and saving Luke's life. "You're all clear, kid. Now let's blow this thing and go home!"

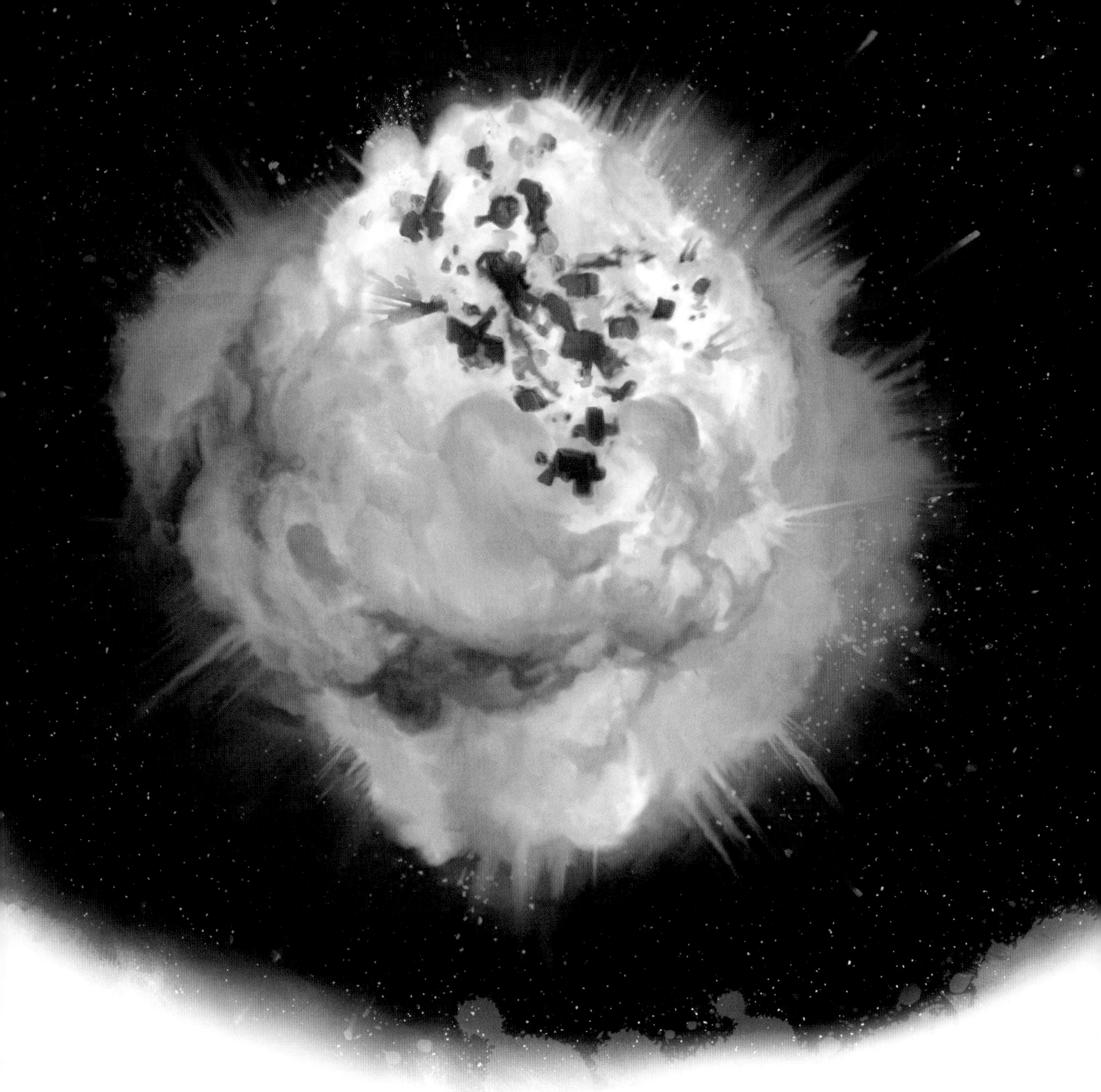

Luke felt the moment align and knew that the Force was indeed with him. Letting it guide his hand, he fired two proton torpedoes into the battle station's exhaust port with perfect accuracy. Just before it could blow up the rebel base, the Death Star exploded in a huge shower of sparks!

"Great shot, kid! That was one in a million!" Han shouted.

But Luke knew better. It wasn't luck. It was the Force.

"Remember, the Force will be with you, always," Obi-Wan's voice said in Luke's head, and Luke knew that, much like the Force, his first teacher would also be with him.

Back on Yavin 4, Luke landed to the rebels' cheers. He was a hero!

Leia ran up, and Luke twirled her in a hug, and then Han was there, too, arms out.

"I knew you'd come back. I just knew it!" Luke told him.

"Well, I wasn't going to let you get all the credit and take all the reward," Han said, ruffling Luke's hair.

"I knew there was more to you than money," Leia told Han as she wrapped an arm around each of them. Luke had never felt so proud in all his life.

It was a whole new experience for Luke, being a hero. Soon he stood on a dais before the entire rebel base, with Han and Chewie on either side, as their new rebel friends cheered their victory. C-3PO waved, and R2 beeped happily. The princess, dressed in a beautiful white gown with her hair in a braided coil, placed a heavy medal around Luke's neck.

The rebels had won the battle.

But the Empire's dark reign was far from over. Darth Vader had survived the Death Star's explosion. The battle station had been destroyed, but Vader and his master, Emperor Palpatine, were already planning their revenge.

THE EMPIRE STRIKES BACK

All across the galaxy, small Imperial probe droids landed on planets and moons, searching for any sign of the Rebel Alliance.

With each passing day, the evil Emperor and his Sith apprentice, the powerful Darth Vader, grew more obsessed with finding their enemies, the determined freedom fighters who had dared to destroy the Empire's dreaded Death Star. But their hunt was also personal, as they sought the young man, Luke Skywalker, who had used the Force to strike at their battle station's only weakness. Through Obi-Wan's teachings and Luke's growing power, the noble Jedi Order lived on, threatening the Emperor's rule. If the Empire could only find the Rebel Alliance and Luke Skywalker, nothing would stand in the way of its ultimate galactic conquest.

The fate of the galaxy hung in the balance as one black probe droid descended to the icy planet Hoth. . . .

Luke Skywalker patrolled the snowy lands around the rebels' hidden Echo Base on the ice planet Hoth, riding a horned tauntaun. The frozen air caught in his lungs. He needed to return to the warmth and safety of the base soon. But just as he was about to turn back, he saw something crash into the snow on the horizon. Was it a meteor? He was about to investigate when his tauntaun grew unsettled.

"Steady, girl. What's the matter?" Luke asked. "Do you smell something?"

Suddenly, a massive white snow beast called a wampa attacked Luke, knocking him unconscious!

Luke awoke hours later. He was hanging upside down from the ceiling of an ice cave as the wampa finished off its tauntaun meal nearby. Just meters away, Luke's lightsaber—the weapon of a Jedi Knight—had fallen into the snow. He couldn't reach it, but he could use the Force, the energy field created by all living things. He stretched out his fingers, and the saber began to wiggle—just as the wampa turned and lumbered toward Luke to continue its feast.

Luke reached out with the Force, and the lightsaber flew into his hand in the nick of time. As the wampa attacked, Luke sliced off the beast's clawed arm with the glowing blade and escaped from the cave. But he was lost in the snow as night fell, and far from safe. He had little chance of survival in such harsh conditions.

Luke fell to the ground, his eyes closing as his body began to freeze. He was about to give up when he saw a vision. It was his old Jedi Master, Obi-Wan Kenobi, appearing to him as a glowing blue Force ghost!

"*Luke, you will go to the Dagobah system,*" Obi-Wan told him. "*There you will learn from Yoda, the Jedi Master who instructed me.*"

"Ben!" Luke reached out for the familiar form, but Obi-Wan's ghost disappeared.

As Luke slipped into unconsciousness, on the verge of freezing to death, a new form appeared: it was his friend and fellow rebel Han Solo, riding on a tauntaun!

Luke woke up back in the rebel base. He was warm again, and a dip in the medicinal bacta tank had healed the damage caused by the wampa and the sub-freezing temperatures. His friends Han, Princess Leia, Chewbacca the Wookiee, and the droids C-3PO and R2-D2 came to check up on him. But Han and Leia soon began to argue. Han said that he was going to leave the rebels to pay off his debt to the crime boss Jabba the Hutt. When Leia told him not to go, Han teased that she liked him, which Chewie thought was hilarious.

"Laugh it up, fuzz ball," Han said, sliding an arm around the princess's shoulders. "You didn't see us alone in the south passage, when she expressed her true feelings for me."

"Why, you stuck-up, half-witted, scruffy-looking nerf herder!" Leia growled, pulling away.

"Who's scruffy-looking?" Han said, pretending his feelings were hurt. "I must've hit pretty close to the mark to get her all riled up like that, huh, kid?" he asked Luke, but Luke looked away and Chewie rolled his eyes.

Leia stepped close to Luke. "Well, I guess you don't know everything about women yet," she told Han as she leaned down to kiss Luke. Luke was stunned, but he didn't complain. He just leaned back and smiled. He knew Han liked Leia, but Luke liked her, too, and . . . well, she hadn't kissed Han.

Luke didn't get to rest for long. The rebels had discovered the Imperial probe droid, which meant that the Imperial fleet knew Echo Base was on Hoth. They needed to evacuate, and quickly.

A fleet of Star Destroyers soon appeared, and Echo Base prepared for a ground assault. The rebels scrambled to their fighters and defenses to hold off the Empire's attack during their evacuation. Even though he had barely healed from his ordeal, Luke was ready to do his part. He hopped in a modified T-47 airspeeder while

Leia commanded the rebel forces from within Echo Base and Han and Chewie struggled to get the *Millennium Falcon* ready to fly.

Overhead, the rebels fired ion cannons at the approaching Star Destroyers as their precious transport ships escaped Hoth's protective shield with starfighters as escorts.

On the ground, white-clad rebels took cover with their blasters as heavily armored AT-AT walkers stomped across the snow bearing weapons of their own, on their way to destroy the Echo Base power generators.

Luke quickly realized that the airspeeders' blasters wouldn't work and encouraged the other rebel pilots to use their tow cables to trip the mighty Imperial walkers. He helped take down an AT-AT, but then his ship crashed in the snow!

Luke knew he had to stop the armored walkers. Shooting a harpoon gun at the belly of an AT-AT, he rose into the air, cut through a hatch with his lightsaber, and tossed a thermal detonator inside, destroying the mighty war machine!

Inside Echo Base, Princess Leia and C-3PO oversaw the evacuation, even as the walls and ceiling shook with each blast.

Han ran into the command room and asked Leia, "Are you all right? I heard the command center had been hit."

Leia turned away to focus on her work. "You've got your clearance to leave."

Han climbed over debris to reach her. "Don't worry. I'll leave. But first I'm gonna get you to your ship."

"Your Highness, we must take this last transport," C-3PO agreed. "It's our only hope!"

As Han tried to pull her away, Leia ordered the rebels to retreat. When word came that Imperial troops had entered the base, Han had finally had enough. Taking Leia's arm, he pulled her from the destroyed room and shielded her with his body as they hurried through collapsing tunnels.

There was one AT-AT left standing, and despite the rebels' bravery, it managed to shoot the generators, destroying any hope of saving Echo Base.

Just as Darth Vader and his snowtroopers stepped into the Echo Base hangar, the *Millennium Falcon* took off! Han, Chewie, Leia, and the droids barely escaped.

As the remaining rebels left on the last transport, Luke watched his friends take off in the Falcon, grateful to know they would be safe. The evacuation was complete. He hopped into his X-wing with R2-D2.

It was time to complete his training.

Obi-Wan Kenobi's Force ghost had commanded Luke to seek out someone named Yoda on the planet Dagobah for further Jedi training. When he reached the right coordinates, however, he was baffled.

"I'm not reading any cities or technology," he told R2. "Massive life-forms, though. There's something alive down there." When R2 beeped apprehensively, he added, "I'm sure it's perfectly safe for droids."

But as he landed, his ship was surrounded by mist. Instead of a clear atmosphere and the landing pads he'd expected, Luke's ship crashed into a wild swamp! Sleens flew overhead, and skeletal trees rose from the fog. The X-wing sank in bubbling green water, and R2 barely escaped the clutches of a hungry dragonsnake.

"Artoo, what are we doing here? It's like something out of a dream. Maybe I'm just going crazy," Luke said. Whoever Yoda was, he was nowhere to be seen. There seemed to be no one on the planet at all.

Luke constructed a camp on the boggy ground, plugged in R2 to charge, and took in his peculiar surroundings. He liked talking to R2-D2 — the droid almost felt like family.

"Now all I've got to do is find this Yoda, if he even exists. It's a really strange place to find a Jedi Master. Still, there's something familiar about this place. I feel like . . ."

"Feel like what?" came a new voice.

Luke spun around, pointing his blaster at a small, ancient alien with big ears, wrinkled green skin, and tufts of white hair.

"Like we're being watched," Luke finished.

The alien cowered, hiding behind his torn brown robes and a twisted walking staff. "Away put your weapon! I mean you no harm. But I am wondering: why are you here?"

Luke lowered his blaster slightly. "I'm looking for someone."

The alien regarded him, his expressive face scrunched up. "Looking? Found someone you have, I would say, hmmm?" And then he cackled, crinkled eyes dancing.

"Right," Luke said, turning away.

"Help you, I can. Yes," the alien urged, ears twitching.

"I don't think so. I'm looking for a great warrior."

"Wars do not make one great." The interloper grunted as he hobbled over to Luke's camp, tossing out spanners and equipment until he found a glowing light, which he refused to return.

"Mine, or I will help you not," he proclaimed.

"I'm not looking for a friend. I'm looking for a Jedi Master," Luke complained.

"Oh! You seek Jedi Master Yoda!" the delighted alien said. "Take you to him I will. Come!"

The alien hobbled off into the swamp with Luke's lamp, and Luke had no choice but to follow, leaving R2 behind to watch the camp.

But Luke's friends had not escaped the Empire so easily.

The *Falcon*'s hyperdrive was damaged, so Han darted into an asteroid field to lose the TIE fighters on their tail.

"Oh, this is suicide! There's nowhere to go!" C-3PO screeched as Han plunged the *Falcon* into a deep, dark hole through the center of an asteroid.

Han shut down the *Falcon* to avoid detection while they worked to fix the hyperdrive.

"You make it so difficult sometimes," Leia told Han as she struggled with a rusty bolt.

"I do, I really do. You could be a little nicer, though," he said, leaning in. "Sometimes you think I'm all right."

"Occasionally. Maybe. When you aren't acting like a scoundrel."

"You like me *because* I'm a scoundrel," Han told her. "There aren't enough scoundrels in your life."

"I happen to like nice men," Leia protested.

"I'm a nice man," Han said, and when he kissed her, she kissed him back.

At least until C-3PO showed up to interrupt them.

Far away, in a secret room, Vader knelt. "What is thy bidding, my master?"

A hologram of Emperor Palpatine appeared, his eyes glowing yellow under the hood that hid his destroyed face. "There is a great disturbance in the Force," he told his apprentice. "We have a new enemy. The young rebel who destroyed the Death Star. I have no doubt this boy is the offspring of Anakin Skywalker."

Vader looked up in surprise. "How . . . is that possible?"

"Search your feelings, Lord Vader. You will know it to be true. He could destroy us."

"He's just a boy," Vader argued. "Obi-Wan can no longer help him."

"The Force is strong with him," the Emperor warned. "The son of Skywalker must not become a Jedi."

"If he could be turned, he would become a powerful ally," Vader offered.

"Yes. He would be a great asset. Can it be done?"

Vader bowed his head. "He will join us or die, Master."

It was raining hard on Dagobah, and Luke had been waiting in the little green alien's mud hut for hours.

"I'm sure your food is delicious, but I don't understand why we can't see Yoda now," Luke said. The food didn't actually smell delicious, but Luke didn't want to be rude.

"Patience! For the Jedi, it is time to eat, as well," the alien replied, bustling around his home.

The ceiling was so low that Luke had to crawl to the pot hanging over the fire, and the alien's stew reminded him of the foul water in the garbage chute on the Death Star.

"Why wish you become Jedi, hmmm?"

Luke tried to eat the food to be polite as he answered, "Mostly because of my father, I guess."

The alien nodded in understanding. "Ah, father. Powerful Jedi was he."

But Luke was fed up with the funny little creature. "Oh, come on. How could you know my father? You don't even know who I am. I don't even know what I'm doing here. We're wasting our time!"

The alien turned his back to Luke and hung his head, whispering, "I cannot teach him. The boy has no patience."

"He will learn patience," a second voice

replied, as if from within Luke's head.

"Much anger in him. Like his father," the alien observed.

"Was I any different, when you taught me?" the voice answered patiently.

The alien turned back to Luke and looked a little sad. "No. He is not ready."

Suddenly, Luke understood.

"Yoda," he said wonderingly, realizing that the funny green alien was in fact the great Jedi Master he'd been sent to find and that the voice in his head was his old master, Obi-Wan Kenobi.

The alien — Yoda — nodded solemnly.

Suddenly, Luke realized how much he could lose. "I am ready," he told Yoda — and the ghost of Obi-Wan, whom he could feel in the Force now. "Ben, I can be a Jedi! I'm ready!"

"Ready, are you?" Yoda asked him. "Adventure. Excitement. A Jedi craves not these things. You are reckless."

"So was I," Obi-Wan reminded him.

Yoda looked up at the ceiling. "He is too old."

"But I've learned so much," Luke protested.

Yoda sighed, his ears drooping. "Will he finish what he begins?"

"I won't fail you. I'm not afraid!"

"Afraid?" Yoda pinned him with a stern glare. "You will be."

Back on the *Falcon*, Han, Leia, and Chewie discovered that the ground inside the asteroid where they were hiding was mushy and the ship was covered in mynocks chewing on the power cables.

"I have a bad feeling about this," Leia said.

When Han shot his blaster at the ground, the entire cave rocked unsteadily. They weren't inside an asteroid. They were inside a massive space worm!

Han, Leia, and Chewie quickly ran back onto the ship and rocketed back up through the cavern – passing through the mouth of the exogorth and out into space right before the gigantic jaws could close and trap them forever!

On Dagobah, Yoda had reluctantly agreed to train Luke. The small alien rode on Luke's back as the young Jedi ran, climbed, and swung through the swamp.

"Yes! A Jedi's strength flows from the Force," Yoda taught. "But beware of the dark side. Anger, fear, aggression – the dark side of the Force are they. Easily they flow, quick to join you in a fight. But if once you start down the dark path, forever will it dominate your destiny. Consume you, it will! As it did Obi-Wan's apprentice."

Luke turned, out of breath. "Vader," he concurred. "Is the dark side stronger?"

Yoda shook his head. "No. But it's quicker. Easier."

"How do I know the good side from the bad?" Luke asked.

"You will know when you are calm, at peace, passive. A Jedi uses the Force for knowledge and defense, never to attack."

Luke knelt and helped the ancient alien off his back. They were deep in the swamp, and their surroundings were unnaturally quiet and dark.

"There's something not right here," Luke said, slipping on his jacket. "I feel cold."

Yoda pointed his cane at the edge of the bog. "That place is strong with the dark side of the Force. A domain of evil it is. In, you must go."

Luke began to fasten on his belt, with his lightsaber and blaster attached, but Yoda stopped him.

"Your weapons. You will not need them."

Luke knew Yoda was a great Jedi Master, but so much of what he said didn't make sense! He buckled his belt on anyway. This planet, he knew, could be dangerous. He went deeper into the swamp, pushing vines out of the way and squelching through the mud. The place — the dark side — called to him, cold but curious. He found a dank hole in the ground and knew that was where he was meant to go. Brushing away lizards and snakes, he crawled down the slippery tree roots and walked toward the source of the icy feeling in his gut.

The Force led him to the remains of an ancient temple, the stone cracked and covered in moss and slime. The air went frigid, and Luke could feel something coming toward him. A tall, dark figure appeared — Darth Vader! Luke backed up and drew his blue lightsaber. Vader ignited his red blade. Vader swung first, and Luke met his every strike. The fight seemed to happen in slow motion until, finally, Luke slashed at Vader, striking his helmet. Suddenly, the helmet's visor exploded, revealing not the twisted visage of a hideous dark lord of the Sith . . . but Luke's own face!

The Force vision troubled Luke, but his training was still incomplete.

Sometime later, Yoda stood on one of Luke's feet while Luke did a one-armed handstand and levitated a rock, practicing his concentration.

"Use the Force," Yoda told him.

But out in the swamp, Luke's X-wing suddenly sank even lower. He panicked, and his concentration broke, sending Yoda and the rock toppling to the ground.

"Oh, no. We'll never get it out now!" Luke said, sloshing toward the last visible corner of his ship.

"So certain are you," Yoda chided. "Always with you it cannot be done."

"Master, moving stones around is one thing, but this is totally different."

Yoda slammed his staff on the ground. "No! No different! Only different in your mind. You must unlearn what you have learned."

"All right. I'll give it a try," Luke said.

Yoda pointed at Luke. "Do. Or do not. There is no try."

Luke concentrated, reaching out with the Force. His ship began to bubble up from the swamp, and R2 beeped encouragement. But then Luke lost his concentration and his grip on the ship, and it sunk all the way down, utterly lost.

His master shook his head sadly.

"I can't. It's too big," Luke whined.

"Size matters not. Look at me. Judge me by my size, do you? Hmph! And well you should not. For my ally is the Force. And a powerful ally it is. Life creates it, makes it grow. Its energy surrounds us and binds us. Luminous beings are we, not this crude matter." Yoda poked Luke in the shoulder; Luke didn't feel very luminous. "You must feel the Force around you. Here, between you, me, the tree, the rock, everywhere. Even between the land and the ship."

"You want the impossible." Luke got up to walk away, but then he heard the water bubbling and R2 beeping excitedly. When he came back, he saw his ship rising from the boggy water as if it weighed nothing. Yoda, his eyes closed, directed it easily to solid ground.

Luke was amazed. "I don't believe it!"

"That," Yoda told him, "is why you fail."

Still, Luke kept on with his Jedi studies. His skills grew, as did his concentration. Soon he could levitate several objects at once — including R2 — while standing on his hands.

"Through the Force, things you will see. The future, the past, old friends long gone . . ." Yoda trailed off expectantly.

As soon as Luke opened his mind, he felt it — his friends were in trouble!

"Han?" he said. "Leia!" His concentration broke, and everything fell to the ground again.

"You must learn control!" Yoda barked.

But Luke was beyond feeling guilty. "I saw a city in the clouds. My friends were in pain."

"It is the future you see," Yoda confirmed.

Luke stood. "Will they die?"

Yoda closed his eyes. "Difficult to see. Always in motion is the future."

"I've got to go to them."

"Decide you must how to serve them best. If you leave now, help them you could, but . . . you would destroy all for which they have fought and suffered."

Luke knew that his master knew best and had more experience with the Force, but his heart told him to help his friends. What use was the Force if he couldn't save the people he cared about? Soon Luke was back in his orange flight suit, preparing his X-wing to leave Dagobah.

"You must complete your training," Yoda reminded Luke. "You must not go."

"But Han and Leia will die if I don't!"

"You don't know that," came Obi-Wan's patient voice. A glowing blue figure appeared behind Yoda: Obi-Wan's Force ghost! *"Even Yoda cannot see their fate."*

Luke stepped forward. "But I can help them! I feel the Force."

"But you cannot control it," Obi-Wan pointed out. *"This is a dangerous time for you. When you will be tempted by the dark side of the Force. It is you and your abilities the Emperor wants. That is why your friends are made to suffer."*

"And that is why I have to go."

Obi-Wan sighed. *"Luke, I don't want to lose you to the Emperor the way I lost Vader."*

"You won't," Luke promised.

"Stopped they must be," Yoda said. "Only a fully trained Jedi Knight with the Force as his ally will conquer Vader and his Emperor. If you end your training now, if you choose the quick and easy path, as Vader did, you will become an agent of evil."

"Patience!" Obi-Wan warned.

"And sacrifice Han and Leia?" Luke asked.

"If you honor what they fight for . . . yes," Yoda answered.

Obi-Wan sadly said, *"If you choose to face Vader, you will do it alone. I cannot interfere."*

"I understand," Luke told him. He dropped his head for a moment, aware of what he was losing but certain of what he was saving. Then he climbed into the cockpit of his X-wing and put on his helmet. Obi-Wan's ghost tried one more time.

"Luke! Don't give in to hate! That leads to the dark side."

"Strong is Vader," Yoda added. "Mind what you have learned. Save you, it can."

"I will. And I'll return. I promise." With that, Luke blasted into space, leaving his mentors behind.

"Told you, I did," Yoda said to Obi-Wan. "Reckless is he. Now matters are worse."

"That boy is our last hope," Obi-Wan said.

"No!" Yoda corrected. "There is another. . . ."

Far away, the *Millennium Falcon* landed on a platform in the floating Cloud City above the planet Bespin. Han needed to repair the *Falcon*, and he hoped his old friend Lando Calrissian would help.

"You've got a lot of guts coming here, after what you pulled," Lando growled, his cape billowing in the wind. But then he stepped close and pulled Han into a tight hug. "How're you doing, you old pirate? So good to see you! What are you doing here?"

"Repairs. Thought you could help me out," Han told him. As Lando had once owned the *Millennium Falcon*, he had a special interest in the ship.

"I'll get my people to work on her," Lando said, leading them inside to a grand apartment where they could get comfortable.

But all was not as it seemed in Cloud City. Lando was handsome and charismatic, but Leia could tell that his easy friendliness was hiding something.

"I've just made a deal that will keep the Empire out of here forever," Lando told his old friend.

Sure enough, when Lando later led them into a dining room to eat, Darth Vader was waiting for them! Han shot Vader with his blaster, but Vader merely deflected the bolts, then used the Force to take the blaster.

"We would be honored if you would join us," Vader said, as if they could do anything else. Soon Han, Leia, and Chewie were surrounded, with stormtroopers on one side and Darth Vader and a bounty hunter named Boba Fett on the other.

"I had no choice," Lando explained. "They arrived right before you did. I'm sorry."

Han reached for Leia's hand. "I'm sorry, too."

They had all been betrayed, and they were immediately imprisoned. After Han was tortured for what seemed like no reason, they realized they were being used as bait.

Darth Vader wanted to capture their friend Luke Skywalker.

But first Vader needed to test a carbon-freezing process to make sure it would work as a way to transport Luke safely to the Emperor. Han would be the test subject, and the bounty hunter, Boba Fett, would then transport Han to the crime boss Jabba the Hutt to claim the high price on Han's head.

Right before Han was put into the carbon-freezing chamber, he asked Chewie to keep Leia safe. In his last moments, Han kissed the princess.

"I love you," she said.

"I know," he answered as he was led away.

Soon Han had been frozen into a solid slab of carbonite.

"See to it that Skywalker finds his way to this chamber," Vader said to his troopers. "Calrissian, take the princess and the Wookiee to my ship."

"You said they would be left under my supervision," Lando argued.

But Vader didn't budge. "I am altering the deal. Pray I do not alter it further."

When Luke landed in Cloud City, he found an empty landing pad and deserted hallways. The first sign of life was Boba Fett leaving, trailed by Han's carbonite slab and Imperial guards. Luke quickly hid and drew his blaster. He didn't need the Force to know that something was very wrong. Luke crept through the white hallways searching for his friends. But when he found Leia and Chewie, their guards fought back.

"Luke, it's a trap!" Leia shouted as they pulled her away.

Still Luke followed.

He wasn't scared for himself; he was worried about her.

Following their trail, Luke ended up in a strange chamber lit blue and red and filled with steam. The lights came on, revealing Darth Vader waiting for him at the top of a set of stairs.

"The Force is with you, young Skywalker. But you are not a Jedi yet," Vader said.

Luke walked up the stairs to face his enemy. Without a word, he ignited his blue lightsaber. Vader ignited his red one, and Luke struck first. It felt just like his vision in the cave!

But instead of holding his own as he had in the vision, Luke was thrown by a fierce strike from Vader. This fight, apparently, would be different. Vader's powers were intense.

"You have learned much, young one," Vader said calmly, as if the fight cost him nothing.

"You'll find I'm full of surprises," Luke responded, attacking with renewed energy.

But Vader's next strike sent Luke's lightsaber clattering to the metal floor. Vader kicked Luke down the stairs, then flew down after him, nearly landing on top of him with his heavy boots.

"Your destiny lies with me, Skywalker," Vader said as Luke unsteadily rose to his feet. "Obi-Wan knew this to be true."

"No," Luke disagreed.

Every time Vader stepped forward, Luke stepped back, until finally he fell down into the carbon-freezing chamber, right where Vader wanted him.

Using his Force powers to initiate the carbon-freezing process, Vader muttered, "All too easy."

But before the process could begin, Luke Force-jumped out of the shaft, so quietly that Vader didn't notice.

"Perhaps you're not as strong as the Emperor thought," Darth Vader said as steam billowed up from the empty chamber. But of course he soon realized his error and turned to find Luke climbing up a tangle of hoses dangling from the ceiling.

He murmured, "Impressive," before swinging his lightsaber, slashing open a hose and barely missing Luke. "Most impressive!"

Luke flipped down to the ground, grabbed the sliced hose, and shot hot steam into Vader's face, using the distraction to snatch up his own lightsaber.

"Obi-Wan has taught you well," Vader said as the duel began anew. "You have controlled your fear. Now . . . release your anger. Only your hatred can destroy me."

They dueled through the steam until Luke pressed Vader off a platform. Luke reholstered his saber and jumped down to end the dark lord of the Sith. They fought again in a control room dominated by a round window looking out onto Cloud City's central air shaft, but Vader distracted Luke again and again, using the Force to pelt the Jedi with pieces of machinery. When one of the pipes broke the window, the vacuum sucked Luke outside, where he hung over the seemingly endless void.

With Lando's help, Leia and Chewie escaped from their Imperial guards and, joined by C-3PO and R2, attempted to save Han from Boba Fett. But they were too late. The bounty hunter blasted off in his ship, *Slave I,* and more stormtroopers arrived. Lando commanded his people to evacuate the city, and the chaos helped Luke's friends retake the *Millennium Falcon.* They zoomed into space with a repaired and working hyperdrive.

But their work wasn't done.

Luke regained his footing but was soon on the run from Vader's lightsaber. Their duel moved over a catwalk, and Vader knocked Luke down onto the narrow metal grate.

"You are beaten," Vader told him. "It is useless to resist. Don't let yourself be destroyed as Obi-Wan did."

The moment Vader mentioned his dead master, Luke felt a new will to fight, felt the anger rise up in him. He leapt to his feet and beat Vader back, sparks flying from their sabers.

But then, with one swift stroke, Darth Vader sliced off Luke's right hand! Luke's lightsaber plummeted down the air shaft as Luke fell to the catwalk, clutching his cauterized wrist. All he could feel was pain and rage, but he fought his anger, knowing such feelings could only lead down the path to the dark side.

"There is no escape," Vader told him, looming overhead with his red lightsaber in hand. "Don't make me destroy you."

On hand and knees, Luke pushed himself away from Vader across a narrow beam.

"Luke, you do not yet realize your importance. You have only begun to discover your power. Join me, and I will complete your training. With our combined strength, we can end this destructive conflict and bring order to the galaxy."

Gritting his teeth against the pain, Luke pulled himself to his feet, clinging to a metal pipe.

"I'll never join you!" he shouted.

Vader held out a gloved hand. "If you only knew the power of the dark side. Obi-Wan never told you what happened to your father."

"He told me enough!" Luke climbed down to a ring of metal, trying to get as far away from Vader as possible. "He told me you killed him."

"No," Vader said, and Luke felt as if even through the mask, the Sith's eyes burned into his heart. *"I am your father."*

Luke clung to the pipe—and to reality.

"No. No, that's not true. That's impossible!" he screamed.

"Search your feelings," Vader told him. "You know it to be true. You can destroy the Emperor. He has foreseen this." Vader made a fist, as if crushing his master. "It is your destiny. Join me. Together, we can rule the galaxy, father and son."

Vader reached out a hand, and Luke considered it. Then he looked down at the air shaft below. On one side was everything he'd ever wanted—a father, a destiny, power, but all tainted by the dark side of the Force. On the other side was possible death—but remaining true to himself, to Yoda, to Obi-Wan, to the valiant fight he'd joined with the rebels.

"Come with me. It is the only way," Vader promised.

But Luke knew it wasn't.

He let go of the pipe and fell down the air shaft.

At first, the shaft went on and on, but then it narrowed, and Luke slipped helplessly down the tube. Soon he was sliding, trying to stop himself, trying to find some way to escape. But then a hatch opened, and Luke fell into the air below Cloud City. He barely caught himself on an antenna, clinging to the slender piece of metal, staring at the solid hull above.

The hatch had closed, and there was no way back in.

The only thing he could do was look to the Force.

"Ben," he begged. "Ben, please."

He waited to hear his old master's voice in his head. So many times, Obi-Wan had spoken to comfort him or push him to try harder. But this time, Ben's voice was silent.

Luke's hand slipped on the metal, and he fell, barely hanging on by his knees. Dangling upside down, running out of energy, bruised and scarred and beaten, still he called out with the Force.

"Ben." It was barely a whisper.

And still Obi-Wan remained silent.

Luke's thoughts went to where his heart led him, and he tried another name.

"Leia. Hear me. Leia."

Luke was so close to letting go when he heard something—a ship. If he could just hold on a little longer, perhaps there was hope. He fell down to the last crossbar on the antenna, and suddenly the *Millennium Falcon* hovered below him. A stranger caught Luke, pulling him down into the ship. Soon Leia was running to him, hugging him close. Somehow, she'd heard him calling through the Force.

But as his friends struggled to get the *Falcon*'s hyperdrive to work again so they could escape the Empire, Luke heard a new voice speak through the Force.

It was Vader.

"Luke."

"Father?" he answered.

"Son, come with me," the voice commanded.

But Luke lay back in his bed on the *Falcon*. He didn't answer Vader.

Instead, he asked, "Ben, why didn't you tell me?"

Still there was no answer. Luke stood and limped to the front of the ship. "It's Vader," he told Leia, watching the giant starship that loomed just outside the viewscreen.

"Luke, it is your destiny," Vader said.

Luke closed his eyes. It would've been so easy to give in. But he wouldn't.

As soon as R2 got the hyperdrive up, the *Falcon* disappeared, and so did Luke's connection with Darth Vader.

His father.

The *Millennium Falcon* rendezvoused with the rebels, and Luke was fitted with a new prosthetic right hand. Lando and Chewie took the *Falcon* to start planning their rescue of Han Solo from Jabba the Hutt's palace on Tatooine.

Luke put his arm around Leia, and together they looked out at the stars. Yoda had been wrong: Luke had saved his friends, but he had not succumbed to the dark side.

He would help rescue Han, then he would keep his promise and return to Dagobah to complete his training. With the Force as his ally, he would defeat Darth Vader and Emperor Palpatine and bring peace to the galaxy. He was sure of it.

RETURN OF THE JEDI

In a galaxy far, far away, a war continued to rage.

Against all odds, the Rebel Alliance struggled to fight the oppressive Galactic Empire and preserve freedom for all. Little did they know that the leader of the tyrannical regime—the evil Emperor Palpatine—along with the dark Sith warrior Darth Vader, worked in secret to complete the rapid construction of a new armored battle station: a second Death Star, even more powerful than the first.

This superweapon would give the Empire ultimate control of the galaxy, and there would be nowhere for the rebels to hide.

However, in the face of these overwhelming odds, one lone Jedi Knight rose to fight the powers of darkness. Luke Skywalker—the son of the great Jedi Anakin Skywalker, who had been lured to the dark side to become Darth Vader—was determined to save the galaxy, and perhaps even his fallen father. But first he needed to rescue his friend and fellow rebel, the smuggler Han Solo, from the vile clutches of the gangster Jabba the Hutt. . . .

Luke Skywalker had always longed for adventure among the stars, but he was back on his home planet, Tatooine, determined to save his friend. Han Solo was frozen in carbonite, heavily guarded in a massive palace belonging to Jabba the Hutt. Luke sent his trusty droids, C-3PO and R2-D2, to the palace with a message for the crime boss.

"Greetings, Exalted One," Luke's floating holo said to Jabba. "I am Luke Skywalker, Jedi Knight and friend to Captain Solo. I know that you are powerful, mighty Jabba, and that your anger with Solo must be equally powerful. I seek an audience with your greatness to bargain for Solo's life."

At that, the huge, sluglike Hutt threw back his head and laughed, as did all the servants and

cronies gathered in his throne room to enjoy music and dancing.

But the holo continued: "With your wisdom, I'm sure that we can work out an arrangement which will be mutually beneficial and enable us to avoid any unpleasant confrontation. As a token of my goodwill, I present to you a gift: these two droids."

"What did he say?" C-3PO shouted worriedly. Luke hadn't told him that part!

"Both are hardworking and will serve you well," Luke's hologram finished before fading out.

Jabba's Kowakian monkey-lizard, Salacious B. Crumb, cackled, but Jabba said in the guttural tones of Huttese, "There will be no bargain. I will not give up my favorite decoration." With one green hand, Jabba gestured to where Han Solo hung on the wall, still frozen in a block of gray carbonite. Jabba would, however, gladly keep the pair of droids.

Later that day, a startling figure appeared in Jabba's presence. A masked Ubese bounty hunter named Boushh had arrived – with Chewbacca the Wookiee bound in chains!

Translating for Jabba, C-3PO told Boushh, "The illustrious Jabba bids you welcome and will gladly pay you the reward of twenty-five thousand credits."

"I want fifty thousand," Boushh replied through a vocoder. "No less."

Furious, Jabba shouted in Huttese and knocked C-3PO over. "The mighty Jabba asks *why* he must pay fifty thousand?" the droid translated.

Boushh answered in Ubese and held out a shining silver globe.

"Because he's holding a thermal detonator!" C-3PO wailed.

Everyone in the throne room dove for safety or covered their eyes, but Jabba just laughed as the detonator's beeps sped up.

"This bounty hunter is my kind of scum – fearless and inventive," Jabba said in his belching language.

Jabba offered the sum of thirty-five thousand credits, and Boushh withdrew the thermal detonator. Chewbacca was dragged away to the dungeon, and the party began again.

Late that night, however, as everyone slept, Boushh crept into the throne room to the wall where Han Solo hung frozen. With the press of a few buttons, the carbonite burned away, and Boushh caught Han as he fell, shivering and blind, to the ground.

"Just relax a moment," Boushh said. "You're free of the carbonite. You have hibernation sickness."

"I can't see!" Han wailed, shaking and weak.

"Your eyesight will return in time. You're in Jabba's palace."

"Who are you?" Han asked, reaching up to touch Boushh's mask.

Boushh removed the mask. It was really Princess Leia in disguise!

"Someone who loves you," Leia said in her own voice.

"Leia!"

She kissed Han and told him, "I've got to get you out of here."

But then Jabba's laughter filled the chamber. The lights came on, and a curtain pulled back to show Jabba and his underlings, who'd been waiting in ambush!

"I was just on my way to pay you back," Han started to explain.

"It's too late to pay me back," Jabba replied in Huttese. "You may have been a good smuggler, but now you're bantha fodder. Take him away."

While Han and Chewie were reunited in the dungeon, Leia was dressed in dancing clothes and forced to sit near Jabba's throne.

It seemed as if all was lost, but then the great metal door to Jabba's palace opened as if by magic and a black-robed figure strode in with great confidence. It was Luke Skywalker! He had used his Force powers to bypass Jabba's guards and servants until he stood directly before the massive Hutt.

"You will bring Captain Solo and the Wookiee to me," Luke said.

Again, Jabba laughed. "Your Jedi mind powers will not work on me, boy."

Luke began to pace. "Nevertheless. I'm taking Captain Solo and his friends. You can either profit by this or be destroyed. It's your choice, but I warn you not to underestimate my powers."

"Master Luke!" C-3PO broke in from behind Jabba. "You're standing on — "

But Jabba spoke over the droid. "There will be no bargain, young Jedi. I shall enjoy watching you die."

As Jabba spoke, Luke caught Leia's eye; she was ready to fight. Off to the side, one of Jabba's guards watched carefully from under an elaborate helmet. It was actually Lando Calrissian. Without another word, Luke used the Force to grab a guard's blaster, but before he could shoot, Jabba hit a button and the floor under Luke fell away. As C-3PO had been trying to tell Luke, he was standing on a trapdoor to a deadly rancor's lair below! Luke tumbled down into the pit, along with one of Jabba's piglike Gamorrean guards.

The moment they landed on the ground, Jabba's throne again slid over the trapdoor overhead, sealing them in. Down in the pit, a metal gate rose slowly, revealing a terrifying rancor—a massive creature with huge teeth and grasping talons. Towering high overhead, the rancor reached for the Gamorrean with a clawed hand and crunched its teeth into the squealing guard. Luke didn't have his lightsaber and could only grab a bone off the floor for self-defense. When the rancor reached for him, Luke wedged the bone in the creature's mouth. Then he picked up a stone and hurled it at a control panel on the wall, which caused the spiked gate to fall on the rancor, crushing it!

Jabba and his friends stopped laughing, but Luke wasn't safe yet. He, Han, and Chewie were to be taken out to the dunes and cast into the Great Pit of Carkoon, the nesting place of the mighty Sarlacc.

"Doesn't sound so bad," Han quipped.

"In his belly, you will find a new definition of pain and suffering as you are slowly digested over a thousand years," C-3PO explained.

Chewie moaned.

"On second thought, let's pass on that," Han said.

But Luke didn't look worried.

"You should have bargained," he warned Jabba. "That's the last mistake you'll ever make."

Jabba's party moved to a pleasure barge so they could watch the upcoming execution. R2-D2 had been assigned serving duty, and he rolled across the barge with a tray of drinks while C-3PO continued translating for Jabba. Leia had no choice but to stay close to the hideous crime lord. Luke, Han, and Chewie stood on smaller skiffs under heavy guard, with their wrists in binders.

Han complained that he was still blind, but Luke told him, "There's nothing to see. I used to live here, you know."

"You're gonna die here, you know," Han said with a shrug. "Convenient."

"Just stick close to Chewie and Lando. I've taken care of everything."

Han didn't believe him, but Luke had developed Jedi skills Han didn't know about yet.

Soon their skiff stopped over a huge hole in the sand that held a monstrous tentacled mouth lined with hundreds of teeth: the Sarlacc!

"Jabba, this is your last chance," Luke called from the edge of the gangplank. "Free us or die."

But, as ever, Jabba laughed, then ordered his guards in Huttese, "Move him into position."

A guard shoved Luke to the end of the gangplank. Luke nodded at Lando, who returned the nod. Then Luke gave R2 a signal.

The guard prodded Luke in the back, and Luke jumped off the gangplank. But instead of plummeting toward the Sarlacc, he spun in the air, caught the gangplank in his hands, and used his Jedi powers to flip back onto the floating craft! Artoo shot Luke's lightsaber out of a secret hatch, and Luke caught it, igniting a green blade and attacking Jabba's guards. He used his new lightsaber to set Han and Chewie free, but when he turned around, he found Boba Fett waiting.

The armored bounty hunter pulled his blaster, but Luke chopped off the barrel. Fett next shot a grappling line around Luke, binding his arms to his sides, but Luke sliced through that, too. With Lando hanging off the skiff and Han still mostly blind, it was up to Luke to jump onto the other craft and start taking out guards. As they worked to rescue Lando, Chewie and Han unknowingly knocked Boba Fett down into the Sarlacc pit!

While all that was happening outside, Leia fought her own valiant battle inside the sail barge. The princess wrapped her chain around Jabba's neck and choked the powerful gangster who had dared to treat her as a slave, ending his cruel reign.

Luke jumped onto the barge, and together he and Leia swung away onto Han and Chewie's skiff to escape. Behind them, Jabba's pleasure barge exploded and plummeted to the sand!

Han was finally safe, but soon the friends were separating again. Han, Leia, Chewie, and C-3PO left on the *Millennium Falcon* to meet with the rebel fleet while Luke and R2 blasted off for Dagobah.

"I have to keep a promise to an old friend," Luke reminded the droid.

As Luke watched his ancient Jedi Master, Yoda, hobble around, it was clear to him that his small green mentor had aged considerably in their months apart.

"Sick have I become." Yoda coughed. "Old and weak."

The wrinkled alien looked down sadly. "Soon will I rest. Yes. Forever sleep. Earned it, I have."

"Master Yoda, you can't die," Luke almost begged.

"Strong am I with the Force, but not that strong. Twilight is upon me, and soon night must fall." Yoda climbed into the ragged blankets of his bed. "That is the way of things, the way of the Force."

"But I need your help. I've come back to complete the training."

Yoda snuggled down and closed his eyes. "No more training do you require. Already know you that which you need."

"Then I am a Jedi," Luke said with great seriousness.

Yoda coughed a laugh. "Not yet. One thing remains—Vader. You must confront Vader. Then, only then, a Jedi will you be. And confront him you will."

Luke had to ask his master one more question.

"Master Yoda, is Darth Vader my father?"

Yoda paused, his back to Luke. "Your father he is. Told you, did he?"

"Yes."

"Unexpected this is." Yoda sighed sadly. "And unfortunate."

Luke bristled. "Unfortunate that I know the truth?"

"No!" Yoda coughed. "Unfortunate that you rush to face him. That incomplete was your training. That not ready for the burden were you." Yoda struggled to breathe.

"Luke. Luke," he whispered. "Do not underestimate the powers of the Emperor, or suffer your father's fate you will."

Luke waited, listening, willing to take whatever knowledge Yoda saw fit to pass on.

"Luke. When gone am I, the last of the Jedi will you be. The Force runs strong in your family. Pass on what you have learned. There . . . is . . . another . . . Skywalker."

With that, the old Jedi's blankets softly collapsed as his spirit joined the Force.

Master Yoda was gone.

As he prepared to leave Dagobah for the last time, Luke knelt beside his trusty astromech droid.

"I can't do it, Artoo. I can't go in alone."

A familiar voice called to him across the swamp: *"Yoda will always be with you."*

"Obi-Wan," Luke murmured as Obi-Wan Kenobi's Force ghost appeared. "Why didn't you tell me? You said Vader betrayed and murdered my father."

"Your father was seduced by the dark side of the Force," Obi-Wan explained. *"He ceased to be Anakin Skywalker and became Darth Vader. When that happened, the good man who was your father was destroyed. So what I told you was true, from a certain point of view."*

"A certain point of view?" Luke repeated.

"Luke, you're going to find that many of the truths we cling to depend greatly on our own point of view."

Obi-Wan's ghost sat down on a log, and Luke joined him to listen. *"Anakin was a good friend. When I first knew him, your father was already a great pilot, but I was amazed at how strongly the Force was with him. I took it upon myself to train him as a Jedi. I thought that I could instruct him just as well as Yoda. I was wrong."*

"There is still good in him," Luke said, almost pleading.

Obi-Wan disagreed. *"He's more machine now than man, twisted and evil."*

"I can't do it, Ben," Luke said.

The ghost was stern but calm. *"You cannot escape your destiny. You must face Darth Vader again."*

"I can't kill my father."

Obi-Wan sighed. *"Then the Emperor has already won. You were our only hope."*

"Yoda spoke of another. . . ."

Obi-Wan turned his ghostly gaze to Luke. *"The other he spoke of is your twin sister."*

Luke looked up in wonder. "But I have no sister."

"To protect you both from the Emperor, you were hidden from your father when you were born. The Emperor knew, as I did, that if Anakin had any offspring, they would be a threat to him. That is the reason your sister has remained safely anonymous."

But Luke already knew who she was. It was as if he'd always known.

"Leia. Leia is my sister!"

With a nod, Obi-Wan confirmed it.

"Your insight serves you well. Bury your feelings deep down, Luke. They do you credit, but they could be made to serve the Emperor."

Luke's mind raced with the possibilities of this new knowledge. He'd always thought himself an orphan, but now he knew the truth: his father and his sister both lived.

And his sister, fortunately, was still within reach.

Meanwhile, Han and Leia rejoined the rebel fleet. The rebels gathered for an important meeting, and their commander, a calm but authoritative human woman named Mon Mothma, spoke.

"The Emperor's made a critical error, and the time for our attack has come," she told them. "Our data pinpoints the exact location of the Emperor's new battle station. We also know that the weapon systems of this Death Star are not yet operational. With the Imperial fleet spread throughout the galaxy, it is relatively unprotected."

A holo of a jagged new Death Star appeared, glowing blood red and still under construction.

"But most important of all, we've learned that the Emperor himself is personally overseeing the final stages of the construction of this Death Star."

Admiral Ackbar, a copper-skinned Mon Calamari, stepped in to explain that the Death Star was protected by a strong energy field generated from the nearby forest moon of Endor.

"The shield must be deactivated if any attack is to be attempted," he told them. The rebel pilots were to fly into the heart of the Death Star and knock out the main reactor.

"General Calrissian has volunteered to lead the attack," Ackbar said.

"Good luck," Han said, smirking at his old friend Lando. "You're gonna need it."

The rebels had stolen a small Imperial shuttle, which would be used to land on the forest moon and deactivate the shield generator.

"Sounds dangerous!" C-3PO warbled.

"Wonder who they found to pull that off," Leia muttered.

When Ackbar asked, "General Solo, is your strike team assembled?" Han looked uncomfortable. He had volunteered!

Chewbacca and Leia immediately agreed to join him on the mission.

"I'm with you, too!" called a new voice, and Luke Skywalker strode into the room. Leia greeted him with a hug.

"What is it?" Leia asked, pulling back to look into his eyes. She could tell something about Luke had changed.

"Ask me again sometime," Luke said, smiling at her. He wanted to tell her that they were siblings, but as Obi-Wan had said, that information could be very dangerous.

Luke, Han, Leia, and Chewie, along with C-3PO and R2-D2, boarded the Imperial shuttle, and soon they were zooming through space on their way to take down the generator.

As they passed an Imperial command ship near the forest moon, Luke stared out the viewport. "Vader's on that ship," he said quietly.

"There's a lot of command ships," Han said. "Keep your distance, Chewie. But don't *look* like you're trying to keep your distance."

Chewie roared in complaint.

"I don't know. Just . . . fly casual," Han told him.

Little did they know that Vader had personally heard their request for clearance to pass the deflector shield to the forest moon. Just as Luke sensed Vader, Vader sensed him, too.

"I shouldn't have come. I'm endangering the mission," Luke said.

"It's your imagination, kid," Han told him. "Let's keep a little optimism here."

Far above, Vader watched their shuttle

bypass the shield . He had plans of his own.

Han's strike force soon landed on the forest moon of Endor.

Clad in helmets and green camouflage capes, the rebels stealthily approached the shield generator hidden in the forest.

Han and Chewie planned to distract the stormtrooper guards, but Han stepped on a stick and caught the troopers' attention. The rebels had been spotted!

A trooper took off on a speeder bike to find help, but Chewie stopped him with a shot from his bowcaster.

Two more troopers escaped on speeder bikes, and Leia and Luke took off together on the remaining speeder to stop them.

Leia was an adept pilot, zigging and zagging between the trees. Luke jumped on one of the other speeders, throwing the trooper off and taking control. Two more troopers followed and began shooting from behind. The trooper Leia was following shot her speeder to the ground right before his exploded against a stump.

Luke took down the final trooper using his lightsaber and returned to the generator. The rebels had prevented the stormtroopers from revealing their position to the Empire, but there was no sign of Leia.

So Luke, Han, Chewie, and the droids ventured into the forest to find her.

Leia awoke to find a small, furry creature standing over her. The creature—an Ewok

named Wicket—cocked his head curiously.

"I'm not going to hurt you," Leia said.

Wicket didn't speak Leia's language, and she couldn't speak his, but—ever the diplomat—Leia soon won Wicket's trust by offering him food.

Wicket settled in right next to Leia to munch on his snack, but when Leia removed her helmet, he scrambled back.

"You're a jittery little thing, aren't you?" Leia teased as she showed him the hat.

But Wicket had stopped in his tracks. He sniffed the air and then scurried under a log.

Sure enough, two stormtroopers stepped into the clearing to capture Leia. But together, Wicket and Leia quickly defeated them.

"Yub, yub!" said Wicket as he took Leia by the hand and led her through the forest.

Luke and his friends followed Leia's trail until it disappeared. Just then, Chewie was enticed by a hunk of meat hanging from a tree. When he touched it, they were all caught in a hanging net—a trap! R2 cut the net and freed them, but it was too late. They were surrounded by Ewoks with weapons, and these Ewoks weren't nearly as friendly and trusting as Wicket.

As soon as the Ewoks saw C-3PO, however, they began bowing and chanting.

"I do believe they think I'm some sort of god!" C-3PO exclaimed.

"Well, why don't you use your divine influence and get us out of this?" Han said.

But the protocol droid was not the commanding type. Soon they were being carried through the forest to a treetop village of ropes and bridges. C-3PO was on a makeshift throne, but the others were tied to branches and dangled over kindling.

"I'm sorry, but it appears you are to be the main course at a banquet in my honor," the droid said from his throne.

Right before the Ewoks lit the kindling, a new figure appeared in the village—Leia! Wicket had taken her back to the village, too, but the Ewoks had welcomed her as a friend.

Leia tried to stop the Ewoks from roasting Han, Luke, and Chewie.

"But these are my friends," she told the Ewoks. When they didn't respond, she looked to C-3PO. "Threepio, tell them they must be set free!"

C-3PO gave the Ewoks a command in their language. The furry warriors ignored him.

Fortunately, Luke had a better idea. "Threepio, tell them if they don't do as you wish, you'll become angry and use your magic."

"But what magic?" the droid asked.

"Just tell them," Luke commanded.

So C-3PO spoke to the villagers in Ewokese, using a scolding voice and many hand gestures. The Ewoks considered C-3PO's words . . . and began to light the bonfires anyway.

But then an amazing thing happened: C-3PO rose into the air on his throne! Luke was using the Force, but the Ewoks saw only the magic of their golden god. They instantly untied Luke, Han, and Chewie and began to treat them with curiosity instead of hostility.

That night, C-3PO further won over the Ewoks with stories of the rebels' victories, and everyone was made part of the tribe. A great celebration began, and the Ewoks agreed to help the rebels in their fight against the Empire.

Away from the celebration, Luke told Leia he needed to leave. "Vader is here. Now, on this moon. I felt his presence. He's come for me. As long as I stay, I'm endangering our mission. I have to face him." Luke paused. "He's my father."

Leia drew back, horrified. "Your father?"

"If I don't make it back, you're the only hope for the Rebel Alliance."

But Leia shook her head. "Luke, don't talk that way. You have a power I don't understand, and could never have."

"You have that power, too. In time, you'll learn to use it as I have," Luke said, hoping she would understand, that she would believe.

"The Force is strong in my family. My father has it. I have it." He looked into her eyes, searching. "And . . . my sister has it."

Leia's face showed doubt, then wonder, then acceptance. "I know. Somehow . . . I've always known."

Luke leaned forward. "Then you know why I have to face him."

Leia stood and spun away, desperate. "No! Run away, far away. If he can feel your presence, then leave this place. I don't understand why you want to confront him."

Luke took her hands. "Because there is good in him. I've felt it. He won't turn me over to the Emperor. I can save him. I can turn him back to the good side. I have to try."

And then he kissed her softly on the cheek and left her alone in the moonlight.

Luke went directly to the Imperial garrison and surrendered himself. He and his lightsaber were delivered directly to Darth Vader.

"The Emperor has been expecting you," Vader told him.

Luke stared straight ahead as they walked side by side. "I know, Father."

"So you have accepted the truth."

Luke turned to stare at him. "I've accepted that you were once Anakin Skywalker, my father."

Vader stopped and tapped Luke on the chest with his own lightsaber hilt. "That name no longer has any meaning for me," he said as a warning.

"It is the name of your true self. You've only forgotten," Luke argued. "I know there is good in you. The Emperor hasn't driven it from you fully. That was why you couldn't destroy me. That's why you won't bring me to your emperor now."

Behind him, Vader ignited Luke's green saber.

"I see you have constructed a new lightsaber. Your skills are complete." Vader turned off the blade. "Indeed you are powerful, as the Emperor has foreseen."

"Come with me," Luke begged him.

"Obi-Wan once thought as you do," Vader said witheringly. "You don't know the power of

the dark side. I *must* obey my master."

"I will not turn," Luke warned him, "and you'll be forced to kill me."

"If that is your destiny," Vader said.

Luke stepped toward the towering figure, clad all in black, trying to make him see.

"Search your feelings, Father. You can't do this. I feel the conflict within you. Let go of your hate."

"It is too late for me, Son," Vader said, almost apologetic—almost sad. But then he caught himself. "The Emperor will show you the true nature of the Force. He is your master now."

"Then my father is truly dead," Luke said sadly as stormtroopers led him away.

Back on the forest moon of Endor, the rebels and their Ewok friends planned to infiltrate the control bunker. When they'd taken down the shield generator from within, the rebel starfighters could attack the Death Star. Fortunately, the Ewoks knew of a secret entrance.

Leia and Han planned a surprise attack, but the Ewoks were already on the move, leading the stormtrooper guards away on a stolen speeder bike. With only one guard left, the rebels abandoned their original plans, taking advantage of the Ewoks' diversion and entering the bunker.

They were in!

Luke, however, was escorted to Emperor Palpatine's throne room on the new Death Star. This was the moment Obi-Wan and Yoda had warned him about, but Luke was confident he wouldn't fall to the dark side.

"Welcome, young Skywalker," the Emperor said as his throne spun dramatically to face Luke. "I have been expecting you. You'll no longer need those."

With a flick of his fingers, the old Sith Lord removed the binders from Luke's wrists.

The Emperor then dismissed his red-clad Royal Guard. It was just Luke, Darth Vader, and the Emperor, whose yellow eyes glowed under the hood of his black cloak.

"I'm looking forward to completing your training," he said. "In time, you will call me master."

"You're gravely mistaken," Luke said calmly. "You won't convert me as you did my father."

The Emperor stood and walked to Luke, looming menacingly for one who looked so old and frail.

"Oh, no, my young Jedi. You will find that it is you who are mistaken about a great many things."

Vader handed Luke's lightsaber to the Emperor.

"Ah, yes. A Jedi's weapon. Much like your father's. By now you must know your father can never be turned from the dark side. So will it be with you."

Luke shook his head. "You're wrong. Soon I'll be dead, and you with me."

But the Emperor just cackled madly.

"Perhaps you refer to the attack by your rebel fleet? Yes, I assure you we are quite safe from your friends here."

"Your overconfidence is your weakness," Luke told him.

"Your faith in your friends is yours," the Emperor spat.

As Palpatine returned to sit on his throne, framed by the stars outside, Vader urged, "It is pointless to resist, my son."

"Everything that has happened has done so according to my design," the Emperor said smugly. "Your friends up there on the forest moon are walking into a trap, as is your rebel fleet. It was I who allowed the Rebel Alliance to know the location of the shield generator. It is quite safe from your pitiful little band. An entire legion of my best troops awaits them."

The Emperor stood, a hideous, cruel grin stretching across his face.

"Oh, I'm afraid the deflector shield will be quite operational when your friends arrive."

On the forest moon, the rebels entered the bunker to take down the shield around the Death Star, but C-3PO and the Ewoks could only watch, helpless, as a new detachment of stormtroopers followed them into the bunker and captured them.

The Emperor's trap had been sprung.

In the space around the Death Star, Lando and the rebel fighter ships arrived and found the shield still up and their signals jammed. They realized that the Empire knew they were coming, and scrambled to escape. Before they could jump to hyperspace, however, hundreds of Imperial TIE fighters filled the sky.

"It's a trap!" Admiral Ackbar shouted.

Laser fire erupted, and Lando struggled to keep his fighters safe. He was flying the *Millennium Falcon*, the fastest ship in the galaxy, but he was in trouble. And so was the entire Rebel Alliance.

From his throne room within the Death Star, Emperor Palpatine called Luke to the window. "Come here, boy. From here you will watch the final destruction of the Alliance and the end of your insignificant rebellion."

Watching ships explode, Luke knew all his friends and allies were in trouble. He looked to his lightsaber, resting beside the Emperor's hand.

"You want this," the Emperor said knowingly, putting possessive fingers on the saber's hilt. "Don't you? The hate is swelling in you now. Take your Jedi weapon. Use it. I am unarmed. Strike me down with it. Give in to your anger. With each passing moment, you make yourself more my servant."

Luke watched the battle outside, then turned back to face the Emperor. "No," he said calmly.

But the Emperor was unconvinced.

"It is unavoidable," he told Luke. "It is your destiny. You, like your father, are now . . . mine."

On the forest moon, Luke's friends were led out of the bunker and found themselves surrounded by stormtroopers, Imperial officers, and AT-ST walkers.

They'd been caught.

The shield generators were still functional and well-guarded.

Now the rebels' plans would surely fail.

Suddenly, Ewoks erupted from the forest, blowing their war horns and shooting arrows! The furry aliens were fierce and fearless warriors, and they attacked the Empire's forces with glee.

In the resulting chaos, Han, Leia, and Chewie grabbed weapons and began shooting alongside their new allies.

As Chewie and the Ewoks took down the stormtroopers and their vehicles one by one using primitive weapons, Han and Leia fought their way back into the bunker to finish what they'd started and take down that shield.

But back on the Death Star, Luke didn't know his friends were still fighting. He only saw the destruction of their plans, and the Emperor could sense his concern and anger.

"As you can see, my young apprentice, your friends have failed. Now witness the firepower of this fully armed and operational battle station." The Emperor pushed a button and said, "Fire at will, Commander."

Luke could only watch helplessly as green lasers emerged from the Death Star, converged into a giant beam of light, and exploded a rebel command ship.

"Your fleet is lost, and your friends on the Endor moon will not survive. There is no escape, my young apprentice. The Alliance will die, as will your friends," the Emperor assured him.

Luke did his best to fight the rage rising in his soul.

"Good," the Emperor moaned. "I can *feel* your anger. I am defenseless. Take your weapon. Strike me down with all of your hatred, and your journey toward the dark side will be complete."

Finally, Luke could stand it no more. He spun around and used the Force to snatch up his lightsaber, igniting the green blade.

But when Luke attempted to strike down the Emperor, his lightsaber's slash was met by Vader's red blade! The Emperor just laughed as the duel continued around his throne room. Every time Luke seemed to have the advantage, the Emperor reminded him to use his feelings, to let his hate flow. But Luke didn't want to do that. He put away his weapon.

"I will not fight you, Father." He backed away as Vader cornered him.

"You are unwise to lower your defense," Vader said, but when he suddenly struck, Luke reignited his weapon. Their sabers crackled and struck again and again, the father and son evenly matched.

Luke flipped up and away to stand over Vader on a metal walkway. "Your thoughts betray you, Father. I feel the good in you, the conflict."

"There is no conflict," Vader argued.

"You couldn't bring yourself to kill me before, and I don't believe you'll destroy me now," Luke said calmly.

"You underestimate the power of the dark side. If you will not fight, then you will meet your destiny."

Vader flung his saber at Luke, who dodged the blade but fell as it cut through the walkway. The Emperor laughed as father stalked son.

"Good. Good!" the old man cried.

Far below on the forest moon, Han and Leia set charges inside the bunker to blow up the shield generator. With the help of the Ewoks, they'd defeated the Emperor's trap. In the space around the Death Star, Lando and his starfighters waited patiently, hiding close to the Empire's Star Destroyers so the Death Star couldn't target them. Lando still believed his old friend Han could shut down the shield, no matter the odds.

"You cannot hide forever, Luke," Vader said as he hunted the shadows, his red saber ready. "Give yourself to the dark side. It is the only way you can save your friends."

He paused.

"Yes. Your thoughts betray you. Your feelings for them are strong. Especially for . . ."

Vader's head swiveled toward Luke.

"Your sister," he said. "So . . . you have a twin sister. Your feelings have now betrayed her, too. Obi-Wan was wise to hide her from me. Now his failure is complete."

Luke tried to fight his feelings, to be calm as Yoda had instructed him. But Vader knew his every weak spot, and Luke's anger burned inside.

"If you will not turn to the dark side," Vader said, "then perhaps *she* will."

That was what finally broke Luke. He had to save Leia.

"No!" he screamed, running at Vader with his green-bladed saber held high.

Their duel continued, wilder and more violent this time. Luke had lost control, just as the Emperor had planned. His strikes pushed Vader back step by step as he beat the Sith Lord to the ground.

Then, with a swift and brutal stroke, Luke slashed off his father's right hand!

Vader's red lightsaber went flying. As Luke stood over his helpless father, green saber aimed at Vader's chest, the Emperor walked toward them, cackling and clapping.

"Good!" he called. "Your hate has made you powerful. Now, fulfill your destiny and take your father's place at my side."

Luke looked down at his own lost hand, at the black glove there so like the ones Vader wore, and then he looked at the smoking wires where his father's hand had been.

"Never," Luke said, throwing his lightsaber aside. "I'll never turn to the dark side. You've failed. I am a Jedi, like my father before me."

The Emperor didn't like that.

"So be it, *Jedi*," he spat.

On the forest moon of Endor, the charges set by Han and Leia worked: the shield generator exploded! The Death Star's shields went down, and Admiral Ackbar commanded his fleet to attack. Lando and his starfighters surged into space, ready to do their duty. For the rebels, the tide had turned.

But for Luke, the battle was far from won.

"If you will not be turned," the Emperor told him, "you will be destroyed."

Raising his withered white hands, the emperor shot Luke with Force lightning.

Luke fell to the ground, writhing, his body alight with pain.

"Young fool. Only now, at the end, do you understand."

More Force lightning arced into the stricken Jedi.

"Your feeble skills are no match for the power of the dark side! You have paid the price for your lack of vision."

Luke screamed as bolt after bolt of lightning burned through his entire body. Vader stood over him, silent.

"Father, please!" Luke begged.

But Vader merely watched calmly as Emperor Palpatine battered Luke with lightning.

"Now, young Skywalker, you will die," the old man growled with grim finality.

Baring his black teeth, the Emperor snarled and began his final blast of Force lightning to kill the young Jedi, once and for all.

Suddenly, Darth Vader picked up Emperor Palpatine and threw him down a shaft at the center of the Death Star!

Luke had been right about his father.

Anakin had risen once more.

He had defeated Emperor Palpatine.

But it would prove to be his final act. Absorbing the Emperor's Force lightning had ruined what was left of his body. His breathing was labored, and the machines could no longer keep him alive.

Deep within the Death Star, Lando piloted the *Millennium Falcon* as he led the rebel fighters toward the reactor core. Rebel ships took out TIE fighters and even a Star Destroyer, which fell to the Death Star's surface and exploded.

They were so close to victory.

They just needed that one, crucial shot.

All Luke could feel was loss.

His father had saved him, but . . . his father was dying.

"Luke. Help me take this mask off," Anakin said.

"But you'll die," Luke protested.

"Nothing can stop that now. Just for once, let me look on you with my own eyes."

Luke took off the layers of the helmet until his father's true face was revealed. Anakin Skywalker was old and pale and scarred, his body twisted by the dark side and destroyed by his battle so many years before with Obi-Wan Kenobi in the lava fields of Mustafar. Still, he smiled to see his son for the first time, face to face.

In a soft voice so different from the one that came from his helmet, Anakin said, "Now go, my son. Leave me."

But Luke would do no such thing. "No. You're coming with me. I've got to save you."

"You already have, Luke. You were right about me. Tell your sister . . . you were right."

With a final smile of hope and contentment, Anakin closed his eyes.

Luke placed his hand on his father's chest. Yes, he'd been right: there had still been good in Anakin Skywalker. But now his father was gone, farther away than he had ever been.

The galaxy, at least, might heal. Luke was not sure if his heart ever could.

Deep inside the Death Star, Lando and his pilots finally reached the generator. Wedge Antilles took one shot, and Lando and Chewie hit the final shot with the *Millennium Falcon*, obliterating their target! They had mere seconds to escape the failing superweapon. So, too, did Luke, who had boarded a stolen Imperial shuttle. They all burst out of range right as the Death Star exploded in a huge ball of fire visible from the forest moon.

The Empire's superweapon was gone, and with it, Emperor Palpatine's reign.

That night, back on Endor, Luke lit his father's pyre, staring into the flames as young Anakin Skywalker had once stared into the funeral flames of Jedi Master Qui-Gon Jinn's pyre. Luke's father had at last turned back to the light side, and therefore he deserved a Jedi's end.

Planets across the galaxy cheered to learn that they were no longer under the cruel control of the Empire. The Rebel Alliance had saved them all, from Naboo to Coruscant to Tatooine.

But Luke, Leia, Han, and their friends celebrated in the small Ewok village on the forest moon of Endor.

Amid the celebration, Luke looked up to see the Force ghosts of his old masters, Obi-Wan Kenobi and Yoda. And then, much to his surprise, a new figure appeared, a young man in Jedi robes, with shaggy brown hair and a warm smile.

It was Anakin Skywalker as he had once been, a proud Jedi Knight!

Luke knew his Jedi Masters—and his father—would always be with him.

The galaxy was at peace. And the Jedi prophecy had finally come true. After so many years, Anakin Skywalker had at last brought balance to the Force.

THE FORCE AWAKENS

Far off, in an unknown galaxy, long-standing peace was slowly splintering apart.

From the ashes of the Empire, a new enemy had risen: the First Order, led by the mysterious Supreme Leader Snoke and a dark warrior of the Force, Kylo Ren. The First Order was determined to restore its own brand of order to the galaxy.

A band of rebels, known as the Resistance and led by General Leia Organa, bravely stood firm in the fight against the First Order's encroaching grasp, but to defeat the mighty evil, they needed to find Leia's brother, Jedi Master Luke Skywalker. After the Emperor's Order 66 during the Clone Wars, the Force-wielding Jedi warriors had become but a legend, and Luke, the last living Jedi, had later disappeared.

But the Force was ever mysterious, and an orphan girl named Rey on the planet Jakku would soon discover that, much like Anakin and Luke Skywalker, she had her own role to play. . . .

A young scavenger named Rey lived alone on the sandy dunes of Jakku.

She had no last name, no friends, and no family. And yet she was tenacious, having built a life for herself in the wreckage of a fallen AT-AT walker sunk in the sand among the ruins of old ships. There was nothing special about her—aside from her will to survive.

Every day, Rey took her salvaged speeder out into the desert to search for parts amid the wreckage, hoping to find something of value. Armed with only a staff, she faced monstrous beasts, greedy scavengers, and harsh conditions. Then she cleaned and fixed her finds and sold them to the junk trader Unkar Plutt for rations in nearby Niima Outpost. Plutt was unfair, but nothing on Jakku was fair.

One day, after selling some old scrap from a long-dead Star Destroyer, Rey heard a strange noise out in the Jakku wastes: nervous beeping. Taking up her staff, she rescued a small, round droid from a fellow scavenger named Teedo.

"He wants you for parts," Rey told the droid after she'd driven off Teedo. "He has no respect for anyone."

The next day, she took the droid, called BB-8, to Niima Outpost with her.

"Don't give up hope. He might show up—whoever it is you're waiting for," she told the droid. "I know all about waiting. My family will be back. One day."

At Unkar Plutt's shop, the blobby junk boss offered Rey sixty portions of food . . . in exchange for BB-8! It was the most food Rey had ever seen, but she refused.

"The droid's not for sale," she told Plutt sternly.

But Unkar Plutt wasn't accustomed to being refused, and he sent his thugs to take BB-8 by force.

Rey was strong from her life among the dunes and unafraid of a fight. She easily repelled the thugs, but BB-8 was too distracted to thank her. He chirped excitedly, telling Rey that a stranger had just arrived wearing his master's jacket.

"What's your hurry, thief?" Rey said as she struck the interloper to the ground with her staff.

"Hey, what?" the man protested. BB-8 had zapped his leg with a small energy prod that extended from the droid's round exterior.

"Where'd you get the jacket?" Rey pressed. "It belongs to his master."

The man sighed in relief. "It belonged to Poe Dameron. That was his name, right? He was captured by the First Order. I helped him escape, but our ship crashed." The man looked directly at BB-8 with pity in his eyes. "Poe didn't make it. I'm sorry."

BB-8 rolled away, sorrowful, and Rey looked more closely at the man, who was young and wearing a brown leather jacket. "So you're with the Resistance?" she asked.

Hope filled his eyes as he stood. "Obviously I'm with the Resistance, yeah."

Rey had never met a Resistance fighter before, but if the man was with them, then she could trust him with the droid's secret. "BB-8 says he's on a secret mission. He has to get back to your base."

"Apparently he has a map that leads to Luke Skywalker," he told her, remembering what Poe had said about the droid before they crashed.

Rey felt a thrill of excitement at that name. "Luke Skywalker? I thought he was a myth."

Before the man could reply, BB-8 rolled up in a hurry, chirping rapidly. He told Rey that First Order stormtroopers were nearby, talking to Unkar Plutt's thugs!

The man in Poe's jacket grabbed Rey's hand and pulled her under an awning as the stormtroopers spotted them and began shooting.

They had to escape!

With BB-8 rolling behind them, they zigged and zagged through the outpost, blaster bolts and First Order TIE fighter laser cannons destroying everything in their wake.

Rey led them toward a quadjumper, but the TIE fighters blew it up. The only ship left was an old piece of junk owned by Unkar Plutt, so they ran up its ramp. Rey sent the man to the guns as she started up the old Corellian freighter, which hadn't flown in years. Rey had always had a gift with machines, from the parts she scavenged to the vehicles and droids she repaired. She had even fixed an old flight simulator so she could practice flying. The ship's cockpit immediately felt like home, and she followed her instincts as she got the hang of the controls. The ship skidded and leapt, but she finally got it in the air.

"Stay low!" the man called from the gun nest

as he looked out on the approaching TIEs. "It confuses their tracking."

Ray flipped the ship around and skimmed over the dunes, dodging the First Order ships. The Resistance fighter was having some problems managing the guns, and without a copilot, Rey couldn't get the ship's shields up. Her only hope was tricky flying. The man managed to take down a TIE, but then his gun got stuck, and Rey had to fly the ship *through* a crashed Star Destroyer, barely escaping a direct hit. Pulling the ship around in a flip, she helped her new friend blast the last TIE fighter so they could escape into space.

Rey knew it was up to her to get BB-8 back to the Resistance before the First Order could capture the droid and obtain the valuable intel about the location of Luke Skywalker. But soon she realized she didn't know the name of the man who was helping her.

"Finn," he told her. "What's yours?"

"I'm Rey."

Finn looked as though he was about to tell her something important, but then a pipe blew, and their attention turned to fixing the ship. BB-8 told them that the Resistance base was in the Ileenium system, and Rey promised to get the droid there safely before returning to Jakku.

Just then, the ship's power cut off and red light bathed everything. They were caught in a tractor beam!

"Someone's locked on to us. All controls are overridden," Rey told Finn.

Their freighter was swallowed by a far bigger ship. Finn was sure it was the First Order. Rey, Finn, and BB-8 hid as she attempted to fill the ship with poisonous gas. But footsteps told them it was too late. Their captors had arrived.

"Chewie, we're home," an older man said.

The Wookiee beside him roared in agreement.

The pair inspected the ship and quickly discovered Rey and Finn.

"Where's the others? Where's the pilot?" the man barked, his blaster aimed at Rey.

"I'm the pilot," Rey told him. "We're the only ones on board."

The man asked them where they'd gotten the ship, and Rey told him that she'd stolen it from Unkar Plutt on Jakku after it had changed hands many times.

"Well, you tell him that Han Solo just stole back the *Millennium Falcon* for good," the man said.

Rey was shocked. Han Solo was a legend from a better time.

"This is the *Millennium Falcon*?" she asked in wonder. "You're Han Solo!"

He shot her a glare. "I used to be."

"Han Solo, the Rebellion general?" Finn asked.

"No, the smuggler!" Rey corrected.

"Wasn't he a war hero?" Finn was confused.

Chewie grunted; Han Solo was all those things.

"This is the ship that made the Kessel Run in fourteen parsecs?" Rey asked, seeing the *Falcon* in a new light.

"Twelve!" Han yelled from the cockpit.

Han wanted to put Rey and Finn in escape pods, but Rey wouldn't let that happen.

"This droid has to get back to the Resistance base as soon as possible," Rey told Han, pointing at BB-8.

"He's carrying a map to Luke Skywalker," Finn added.

At that, Han finally stopped, his back turned to Rey and Finn.

"You *are* the Han Solo that fought with the Rebellion," Finn said, finally starting to believe. Han slowly turned around to face them. "You knew him."

Han grinned. "Yeah, I knew him. I knew Luke."

Rey couldn't believe that the larger-than-life legends were real, and she had so many questions, but Han heard a sound outside of the ship and looked worried.

"Don't tell me a rathtar's gotten loose," Han said before turning and running for the *Falcon*'s ramp.

Finn's eyes went wide as he, Rey, and Chewie followed Han out into the hangar of the larger ship. Rathtars were deadly tentacled monsters.

"Oh, great." Han sighed. "It's the Guavian Death Gang. Must've tracked us from Nantoon."

Han opened a hatch in the floor and pointed at Rey and Finn. "Get below and stay there until I say so, and don't even think about taking the *Falcon*."

"What about BB-8?" Rey pressed.

"He stays with me until I get rid of the gang, and then you can have him back and be on your way."

"What are you going to do?" Rey asked Han.

Han shrugged. "Same thing I always do. Try to talk my way out of it."

Chewie muttered something under his breath.

"Yes, I do!" Han said, shaking a finger at the Wookiee. "Every time."

Soon the Guavian Death Gang, five identical

figures in red suits and masks, and their leader marched down the hall carrying hefty guns while a ragged group of pirates known as Kanjiklub entered the hall from the other direction. Han, Chewie, and BB-8 were trapped by not one but *two* unhappy gangs. Han owed them both money . . . money he didn't have.

"That BB unit," a gang member named Bala-Tik shouted. "The First Order is looking for one just like it. And two fugitives."

Listening from their hiding place belowdecks, Rey knew she and Finn had to act soon.

"If we close the blast doors in that corridor, we can trap both gangs," Rey whispered as she inspected an access panel nearby. "Resetting the fuses should do it."

Unfortunately, Rey selected the wrong fuses. Instead of opening the blast doors, she had released three rathtars!

"I've got a bad feeling about this," Han said, hearing the monsters' screeches.

"Kill them and take the droid!" Bala-Tik ordered.

But his next commands were lost as a huge, hideous rathtar rolled into the hallway and attacked him. Blasters were useless against the tentacled blobs and their toothy maws.

Han and Chewie ran away, with BB-8 rolling behind them, dodging enemies and monsters, and Rey and Finn climbed up onto the deck and ran to help.

"This way," Finn said, leading Rey down a hallway. But a rathtar tentacle whipped out and grabbed Finn's legs, dragging him out of sight.

Rey had to help her friend! She ran to a bank of video monitors and, carefully tracking the rathtar's progress, closed a door just in time to chop off the tentacle that held Finn. He was free!

"It had me — but the door — " Finn stuttered.

"That was lucky," Rey said. Then they were running again, this time out of the rathtar-riddled hallways and back to where the *Millennium Falcon* sat in the hangar. Han, Chewie, and BB-8 had the same idea. Han and Rey ran up the ramp to the *Falcon*'s cockpit as Finn helped Chewie, who'd taken a shot from one of the Kanjiklub pirates.

As Han and Rey both focused on the ship's controls, a giant form engulfed the cockpit window — a rathtar! It fought to break the glass with its mouth, furiously trying to get at the people within.

"This is not how I thought this day was gonna go," Han muttered. "Hang on!"

The *Falcon* lifted off with the ravenous rathtar still wrapped around the cockpit, but the monster soon disintegrated as the ship jumped into hyperspace.

Little did they know that back on Han's old ship, Bala-Tik had survived the rathtars.

"Inform the First Order that Han Solo has the droid they want, and it's aboard the *Millennium Falcon*," he said into his comm.

Meanwhile, Kylo Ren and First Order officer General Hux stood before a hologram of the Supreme Leader of the First Order, the mysterious and powerful Snoke. Snoke's face was twisted and stretched, as if he'd suffered some grievous wound, but nothing about him was weak.

"The droid will soon be delivered to the Resistance, leading them to the last Jedi," Snoke said. "If Luke Skywalker returns, the new Jedi will rise."

"The weapon is ready," Hux told Snoke, speaking of the deadly First Order Starkiller that could destroy an entire planetary system. "I believe the time has come to use it. We shall destroy the government that supports the Resistance: the Republic. Without their friends to protect them, the Resistance will be vulnerable, and we will stop them before they reach Skywalker."

Hearing this, Snoke settled back on his throne. "Go. Oversee preparations."

Once they were alone, Snoke told Kylo, "There's been an awakening. Have you felt it?"

"Yes." Kylo's voice was muffled and dull through his black-and-silver mask.

"There's something more. The droid we seek is aboard the *Millennium Falcon* in the hands of your father." Snoke paused and leaned toward him. "Han Solo."

Kylo looked up at his leader, his emotions, as ever, hidden behind his mask. "He means nothing to me."

Snoke held out a hand. "Even you, master of the Knights of Ren, have never faced such a test."

"By the grace of your training, I will not be seduced," Kylo assured Snoke.

But Snoke only said, "We shall see," before his hologram disappeared, leaving Kylo Ren alone in the echoing chamber.

Back on the *Millennium Falcon*, BB-8 revealed the secret map he'd been hiding, the one that led to Luke Skywalker. The three-dimensional hologram filled the room with planets and stars, plus a dotted line that seemed to go nowhere.

"This map's not complete," Han said. "It's just a piece. Ever since Luke disappeared, people have been looking for him."

"Why did he leave?" Rey asked.

"He was training a new generation of Jedi. One boy, an apprentice, turned against him. Destroyed it all. Luke felt responsible. He just . . . walked away from everything."

"You know what happened to him?" Finn asked.

Han shrugged. "A lot of rumors. People that knew him best think he went looking for the first Jedi temple."

Rey stood, hope fluttering in her chest again. "The Jedi were real?" she asked softly.

"I used to wonder about that myself," Han confided. "Thought it was a bunch of mumbo jumbo. A magical power holding together good and evil, the dark side and the light. Crazy thing is" — Han turned slowly and looked Rey directly in the eyes — "it's true. The Force. The Jedi. All of it. It's all true."

Rey felt a strange connection to the man and to his stories, and she wanted so much to believe him, to believe in the mystical Jedi. But the ship started beeping, so BB-8 shut off the hologram as Han headed for the controls.

"This is our stop," he told Rey.

Below them, Takodana had appeared, sparkling blue and green like a jewel.

"I didn't know there was this much green in the whole galaxy," Rey said, amazed and entranced to see a place so different from the hard, dusty world of Jakku.

Han landed the *Falcon* near a castle on the edge of a lake. Rough stone turrets and walls rose up among the trees. As Rey stood by the water, marveling, Han handed her a small blaster and said, "You might need this."

"I think I can handle myself."

"I know you can. That's why I'm giving it to you. You know how to use it?"

Rey aimed the blaster at a stump. "Yeah, you pull the trigger."

Han pushed her arm down. "Little bit more to it than that. You got a lot to learn." He paused, considering. "You got a name?"

"Rey."

"Rey," he repeated. "Look, I been thinking about bringing on some more crew. A second mate. Someone to help out. Someone who can keep up with Chewie and me, who appreciates the *Falcon* . . ."

Rey moved in front of him, giddy with excitement. "Are you offering me a job?"

"I wouldn't be nice to you," Han grumbled. "Doesn't pay much."

"You're offering me a job!"

Han shook his head. "I'm thinking about it."

But Rey looked down, and guilt settled like a stone around her neck. "If you were, I'd be flattered. But I have to get home. I've already been away too long."

Han watched her carefully. "That's too bad. Chewie kind of likes you."

Rey had spent so much time on Jakku waiting and hoping for her family to return. She wasn't about to give up now.

Soon they were marching up a dirt path through lush green grass, toward the ancient stone castle. Han told them they needed to find a nondescript ship to get BB-8 safely back to the Resistance. The *Falcon* was just too easy to find.

"Maz Kanata's our best bet," Han said as they passed into a courtyard festooned with brightly colored flags from all planets and creeds. "She's run this watering hole for a thousand years. She's a bit of an acquired taste, so let me do the talking." He paused before the heavy wooden doors and looked back. "And whatever you do, don't stare."

"At what?" Rey and Finn asked at the same time.

Han waved his arms. "Any of it!"

The doors opened to reveal a busy cantina

and restaurant. All kinds of aliens were playing games of chance, eating, drinking, enjoying the live music, and watching one another with shifty eyes.

Rey couldn't help it – she definitely stared. She'd never seen any place like Maz's castle.

Unbeknownst to Rey and her friends, two beings had noticed their arrival. One, an unassuming old serving droid, picked up a radio and communicated, "Alert the Resistance. Their missing droid is here!" The other, unfortunately, was not so altruistic. Bazine Netal, a slender bounty hunter clad in a black-and-white ensemble, found a quiet place to make her call.

"Inform the First Order . . . I've found the droid."

On the First Order's Star Destroyer, the *Finalizer*, Kylo Ren knelt alone in his chamber.

Before him sat the burned, twisted helmet of Darth Vader.

"Forgive me," Kylo said, his voice tight with feeling. "I feel it again. The pull to the light. Supreme Leader senses it. Show me again the power of the darkness, and I will let nothing stand in our way."

He looked up. "Show me, Grandfather, and I will finish what you started."

Back on Takodana, Han introduced Finn and Rey to Maz, a small alien with a wrinkled, golden face and intelligent eyes magnified by huge lenses.

"I assume you need something," Maz said to Han as she led them to an empty table.

"Maz, I need you to get this droid to Leia," Han said.

Maz considered it, grinning, and finally said, "Hmmm . . . no. You've been running away from this fight for too long. Han, go home."

"Leia doesn't want to see me," Han muttered.

"What fight?" Rey asked.

Maz looked at her intently. "The only fight. Against the dark side. Through the ages, I've seen evil take many forms. The Sith. The Empire. Today it is the First Order. Their shadow is spreading across the galaxy. We must face them. *Fight* them. All of us."

But Finn interrupted her, saying, "There is no fight against the First Order. Not one we can win. I bet you the First Order is on their way right now."

Maz focused on him. "I'm looking at the eyes of a man who wants to run."

"You don't know a thing about me," Finn replied. "Where I'm from. What I've seen. You don't know the First Order like I do. They'll *slaughter* us. We all need to run."

Maz pointed to a red-cloaked mercenary and a turtle-like alien with a pointed peg leg.

"You see those two? They'll trade work for transportation to the Outer Rim. There, you can disappear."

Rey couldn't believe Finn would just run, after what he'd seen. "Finn! What about BB-8? We have to get him back to your base."

But Finn gave her a sad, searching look.

"I'm not who you think I am," he said. "I'm not Resistance. I'm not a hero." He paused. "I'm a stormtrooper. Like all of them, I was taken from a family I'll never know. And raised to do one thing. In my first battle, I made a choice. I wasn't going to kill for them. So I ran. I helped Poe escape and ran right into you. And you looked at me like no one ever had. But I'm done with the First Order. I'm never going back. Rey, come with me."

She was floored—and disappointed. But she wasn't going to give up on him. "Don't go," was all she could say.

Finn shook his head sadly and said, "Take care of yourself. Please," before leaving with the mercenaries.

As Rey watched Finn go, tears in her eyes, she felt something pulling her toward a winding set of stone stairs. She soon entered a room filled with old junk. Trunks, spare parts, and mysterious artifacts beckoned, but Rey's feelings led her straight to a small wooden chest. When she knelt and opened it, she found a strange metal object.

The moment she touched it, the world plunged into darkness as if Rey were dreaming. She heard heavy breathing, amplified as if through a mask. She saw visions of rain, lightning, and the red light of a fire shining on a white-and-blue astromech as a hooded figure placed a metal hand on the droid. She heard screams and saw a battle. A figure in a black-and-silver mask, holding a red, glowing blade, faced her, flanked by armor-clad warriors. Then she saw herself, just a girl, being dragged away by Unkar Plutt on Jakku as a ship blasted off into the sky—it was the moment her parents had left her. But the scene changed again, and she was in a forest, running through black trees as the masked figure with the red lightsaber appeared, blocking her path, hunting her, his weapon buzzing menacingly. She stumbled back, landing on the rocky floor of Maz's castle as the vision disappeared.

Maz stood nearby, watching her.

"What was that?" Rey asked, still breathing hard and near tears from all she'd seen, all she'd felt—fear, loss, pain, sadness, loneliness, betrayal, terror.

Maz put up a hand to quiet her. "That lightsaber was Luke's. And his father's before him. And now, it calls to you."

But Rey shook her head. "I have to get back to Jakku."

Maz nodded knowingly. "Dear child. Whoever you're waiting for on Jakku, they're never coming back. The belonging you seek is not behind you, it is ahead. I am no Jedi, but I know the Force. It moves through and

surrounds every living thing. Feel it. The light . . . it's always been there. It will guide you. The saber. Take it."

Rey scrambled to her feet.

"I'm never touching that thing again! I don't want any part of this."

She turned and ran out of the castle and into the forest toward the *Falcon*.

Across space, General Hux gave a rousing speech to his amassed forces.

"Today is the end of the Republic," he growled. "The New Republic lies to the galaxy while secretly supporting the treachery of the loathsome Resistance. This fierce machine which you have built, upon which we stand, will bring an end to the Senate, to their cherished fleet. All remaining systems will bow to the First Order and will remember this as the last day of the Republic."

The stormtroopers and officers saluted him, and he shouted, "Fire!"

The sky turned red as a great beam of energy shot out of the planet they called Starkiller Base. Arcing through space, the red beam drew attention from beings on every planet it passed, even stopping Finn as he left Maz's castle on Takodana.

But on the planet Hosnian Prime, where the New Republic's Senate met, the beam did not just fly past. It grew bigger and bigger until it struck the planet, obliterating the Senate and every life-form in the entire Hosnian system!

As General Hux had assured his troops, the New Republic was gone.

Meanwhile, Rey ran through the forest on Takodana – although she wasn't sure if she was running from her past or her future. The visions she'd seen had shaken her to her core. Suddenly, ships screamed by overhead: it was the First Order!

Rey watched in horror as the grand stone towers of Maz's castle crumbled under the First Order's laser fire. Stormtroopers appeared, aiming right at her. She managed to shoot several with Han's blaster, but more appeared, chasing her deeper into the forest.

"You have to keep going," she told BB-8, who had followed her. "I'll try to fight them off." The little droid hesitated, but then rolled away obediently.

Back at the castle, Finn had seen the First Order arrive and hurried back to find Rey. Maz gave him Luke's lightsaber, urging him to give it to Rey when they met again. But when Finn went outside, a trooper called out to him, "Traitor!"

It was one of the stormtroopers from his old squadron, ready for a fight. Armed with the saber, Finn fought off the trooper but was eventually cornered, along with Han and Chewie, by other soldiers. Maz's castle was reduced to rubble, and it seemed that all was lost . . . until a squadron of Resistance ships arrived! They engaged the First Order ships and took out the stormtroopers clustered around what was left of the castle, allowing Finn, Han, and Chewie to escape.

As for Rey, she hid in the woods, but soon she heard the distinctive hum of a lightsaber. The helmeted figure from her vision stepped out from behind a boulder, his red lightsaber drawn! She blasted him again and again, but he batted the bolts away with his saber as he stalked her through the forest. As if finally bored by her self-defense, the figure held up a hand, and Rey's entire body froze, her blaster arm pinned down. Try as she might, she couldn't move as the black-cloaked figure strode toward her.

"The girl I've heard so much about," the figure said, his voice flat through the helmet. "The droid." He held the red saber blade centimeters from her face. "Where is it?"

Rey tried to turn away but couldn't; she couldn't do anything.

The figure held up a black-gloved hand, almost touching her face. "The map," he whispered. "You've seen it!"

Stormtroopers arrived, but the figure told them to withdraw.

"Forget the droid. We have what we need."

With a wave of his hand, Rey fell unconscious, and they carried her away.

At the remains of Maz's castle, a Resistance transport landed amid the rubble. The last person out of the ship was an older woman with gray hair swept up in a graceful braided crown. When she saw Han, she stopped and smiled. But before she could speak, a shiny gold protocol droid stepped in front of her.

"Goodness!" he exclaimed cheerfully. "Han Solo! It is I, C-3PO." He turned back to the older woman. "Look who it is! Did you see — "

The woman gave him a knowing look, and C-3PO said, "Oh! Excuse me, Prin — General. Sorry. Come along, BB-8."

Without the two droids standing between them, General Organa, once known as Princess Leia, stood facing Han Solo.

"You changed your hair," he said.

"Same jacket," she responded, inclining her head at Han.

"No! New jacket."

But Chewie didn't stand apart. He stepped close, roaring gently and sweetly, and drew his old friend Leia into a hug.

After Chewie walked away, Han finally met Leia's eyes and said, softly, "I saw him. Leia, I saw our son. He was here."

Ben Solo, Han and Leia's son, had trained with Luke to become a Jedi. But Snoke had twisted his heart to the dark side, and now he was known by another name: Kylo Ren.

Han, Chewie, Finn, BB-8, and the Resistance returned to a secret base on the planet D'Qar. As soon as they landed, BB-8 rolled out of the ship in a hurry. Finn couldn't believe his eyes — the droid was racing toward Poe Dameron!

"BB-8, my buddy!" Poe greeted his droid. "It's so good to see you!"

Finn and Poe were also glad to see each other

again, after their daring escape from the First Order and the terrible crash that had separated them on Jakku. Together, they hurried to the underground command center where the Resistance was preparing its battle plans. Finn had worked as a stormtrooper on the Starkiller Base that had destroyed the Hosnian system, and he was sure that was where the First Order had taken Rey.

Leia promised to help, but first she needed to know everything. They began by looking at the map carried by BB-8. The map was incomplete, but BB-8 did not give up so easily. The plucky droid rolled over to another astromech droid who could help, R2-D2!

"R2-D2 has been in low-power mode ever since Master Luke went away," C-3PO explained to BB-8. "Sadly, he may never be himself again."

Across the room, Han spoke gently to Leia about their son.

"There's nothing more we could've done," he assured her. "We lost our son. Forever."

"No," Leia disagreed. "We can still save him. Me. You."

But Han wasn't convinced. "If Luke couldn't reach him, how could I?"

Leia's eyes shone with love and conviction. "Luke is a Jedi. You're his father. There is still light in him. I know it."

Rey awoke in an interrogation chair, her arms and legs shackled.

"Where am I?" she asked.

Kylo Ren squatted nearby, watching her.

"You're my guest," he replied.

"Where are the others?"

"Do you mean the murderers, traitors, and thieves you call friends? You'll be relieved to hear I have no idea."

With that, Kylo removed his helmet and walked a slow circle around Rey.

"Tell me about the droid," he said.

"He's a BB unit with a selenium drive and a thermal hyperscan vindicator — " Rey began.

"It's carrying a section of a navigational chart," Kylo said. "And we have the rest, recovered from the archives of the Empire. But we need the last piece, and somehow you convinced the droid to show it to you."

When she didn't respond, Kylo shook his head in disgust. "You know I can take whatever I want." He put a hand near her head, as if to draw out the information. "You're so lonely," he observed.

A tear fell down Rey's cheek.

"You imagine an ocean. I see the island. And Han Solo. You feel like he's the father you never had. He would've disappointed you."

"Get out of my head," Rey snapped.

Kylo pulled away. "I know you've seen the map. It's in there. And now you'll give it to me." Then, softer, "Don't be afraid. I feel it, too."

When he held out his hand again, Rey fought his grip. "I'm not giving you anything."

He gave her a pitying smile and said, "We'll see."

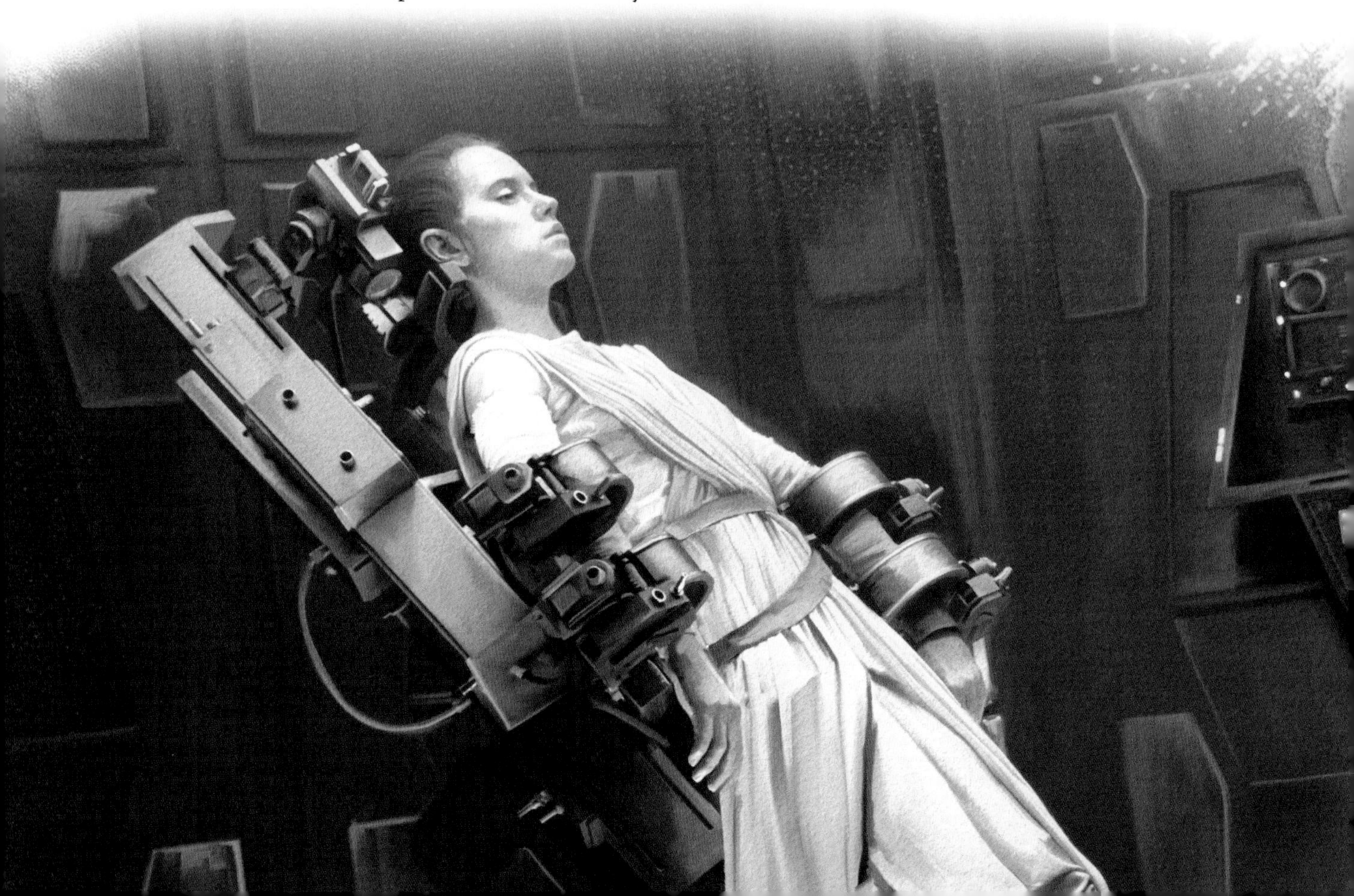

Rey gritted her teeth and pulled down walls in her mind. Kylo doubled down, making eye contact and reaching deeper. Rey turned it around, pushing the barrier from her mind . . . and into his!

"You," she growled. "You're afraid — that you will never be as strong as Darth Vader!"

Kylo whipped his arm away, stepped back, and left the chamber.

She had scared him.

Rey struggled against her restraints before realizing that perhaps her new powers could help her escape.

"You will remove these restraints and leave this cell with the door open," she said to her stormtrooper guard.

"What'd you say?" he asked.

With hope in her heart, she repeated the phrase, but he just barked, "I'll tighten those restraints, scavenger scum!"

As she stared at him, knowing that Kylo Ren would soon return, she felt a sense of calm and certainty wash over her. In a new voice completely free of doubt, she repeated, "You will remove these restraints and leave this cell with the door open."

After a brief pause, the guard calmly replied, "I will remove these restraints and leave the cell with the door open."

And he did!

As he walked out the door, Rey added, "And you'll drop your weapon."

"And I'll drop my weapon."

As his footsteps receded, Rey scrambled out of the chair and picked up the blaster.

Back on D'Qar, the Resistance discussed ways to destroy Starkiller Base. A holo showed that it was much larger than the Death Stars had been.

"How is it possible to power a weapon of that size?" Admiral Ackbar asked.

"It uses the power of the sun," Finn informed them. "As the weapon is charged, the sun is drained until it disappears."

"The First Order is charging the weapon again now," General Organa said calmly. "Our system is the next target."

"Oh, my," C-3PO said. "Without the Republic fleet, we're doomed."

"Okay, how do we blow it up?" Han asked. "There's always a way to do that."

"Han's right," Leia said.

"It would have to have some kind of thermal oscillator," a Resistance officer observed.

"There is one." Finn hurried around to point at the holo. "Precinct forty-seven. Here."

"If we can destroy that oscillator, it might destroy the core and cripple the weapon."

Poe was getting excited. "We'll go in there and hit that oscillator with everything we've got!"

"But they have defensive shields that our ships cannot penetrate," Ackbar reminded them.

"We disable the shields," Han said. After all, he'd done it before, with the second Death Star.

He looked to Finn. "Kid, you worked there. What have you got?"

"I can do it," Finn said.

Han pointed at him and smiled. "I like this guy."

"I can disable the shields, but I have to be there," Finn added. "On the planet."

Han looked to Chewie, who nodded. "We'll get you there."

"You know, no matter how much we fought, I've always hated watching you leave," Leia said as Han checked the *Falcon*.

Han grinned. "That's why I did it. So you'd miss me."

Leia returned his grin. "I did miss you."

"It wasn't all bad, was it?" Han asked her. "Some of it was good."

Leia chuckled. "Pretty good."

Han stepped closer. "Some things never change."

Leia stepped closer, too. "True. You still drive me crazy."

Han sighed and pulled her into a hug, her head pressed to his heart.

"If you see our son," she murmured, "bring him home."

The *Millennium Falcon* left hyperspace and nearly crashed into Starkiller Base, skimming over the trees and skidding across the snow to avoid detection. Han, Finn, and Chewie approached a flooding tunnel to sneak in.

"What was your job here?" Han asked.

"Sanitation," Finn answered.

Furious, Han grabbed Finn's jacket. "Sanitation? Then how do you know how to disable the shields?"

"I don't," Finn answered unapologetically. "I'm just here to get Rey."

"People are counting on us. The galaxy is counting on us!"

"We'll figure it out," Finn said calmly. "We'll . . . use the Force."

"That's not how the Force works!" Han growled.

But Finn just ran down the tunnel, calling "Come on!" over his shoulder.

Overhead, a hot white beam of light from the sun was being absorbed by the base. Soon the weapon would be charged and ready to blow up D'Qar—and the entire Resistance fleet.

Finn led Han and Chewie into the base. He had an idea about how to get the shields down. As Captain Phasma, the commander of the First Order's legion of stormtroopers, passed on her rounds, her chrome armor shining and cape snapping, Chewie lunged out of a dark hallway and grabbed her.

"You remember me?" Finn asked after they'd secured her.

"Eff-Enn-Two-One-Eight-Seven," she said crisply.

"Not anymore. The name's Finn, and I'm in charge now, Phasma! So follow me."

Han and Chewie led Phasma to the shield

data screen at blaster point, where Finn ordered her to lower the shields.

"You're making a big mistake," Phasma told him.

"Do it," Finn responded.

Much to his surprise . . . she began typing.

"Solo, if this works, we're not gonna have a lot of time to find Rey," Finn said.

"Don't worry, kid," Han replied. "We won't leave here without her."

The shield went offline, and Phasma stood. "You can't be so stupid as to think this will be easy. My troops will storm this block and kill you all."

"I disagree," Finn said. "What do we do with her?"

Han grinned, recalling his own trip to the Empire's first Death Star, long before.

"Is there a trash compactor?" he asked.

Finn grinned, too. "Yeah, there is."

Back on D'Qar, the Resistance learned that the Starkiller's shields were down and ordered the starships, led by Poe Dameron, to fire on the vulnerable oscillator. The X-wings screamed out of lightspeed and approached their target.

But the First Order was ready. "Dispatch all squadrons," Hux commanded.

One of Poe's ships scored a direct hit on the oscillator, but nothing happened.

"We gotta keep hitting it," Poe told his squad. "Another bombing run. Remember, when the sun is gone, that weapon will be ready to fire. But as long as there's light, we've got a chance."

On Starkiller Base, with Phasma sent down the garbage chute, Finn and Han argued about how to find Rey and escape before the superweapon blew up. But Han spotted something: Rey climbing up part of the ship as she escaped on her own!

"What happened? Did he hurt you?" Finn asked her. "We came back for you."

Chewie roared.

"What'd he say?" Finn asked.

"That it was your idea." Rey hugged him, hard, and thanked him. No one had ever come back for her before.

"How did you get away?" Finn asked her.

She pulled back. "I can't explain it. And you wouldn't believe it."

"Escape now, hug later," Han reminded them.

Overhead, the battle raged as the Resistance fighters sought to bombard the oscillator while under attack by First Order ships.

"We've got a bag full of explosives. Let's use them," Han said.

Han and Chewie took the explosives while Rey and Finn accessed the controls to open all the doors that stood between their friends and the oscillator the starfighter pilots were trying so hard to hit.

Han handed Chewie the detonator that would explode the charges and told him, "We'll meet back here."

Chewie climbed to a higher catwalk and began planting his explosives while Han went to a lower level and did the same.

But Kylo Ren had felt his father in the Force and brought his stormtroopers to find and stop Han Solo. As Kylo walked out onto a catwalk, Han crept out of his hiding place, remembering Leia's only request.

"Ben!" he shouted.

Kylo stopped on the catwalk.

"Han Solo. I've been waiting for this day for a long time."

Han walked out onto the catwalk to meet him. "Take off that mask. You don't need it."

"What do you think you'll see if I do?"

"The face of my son."

Kylo Ren removed his helmet. "Your son is

gone. He was weak and foolish like his father, so I destroyed him."

Han stepped closer. "That's what Snoke wants you to believe. But it's not true. My son is alive."

"No. The Supreme Leader is wise."

"Snoke is using you for your power. When he gets what he wants, he'll crush you."

They were face to face, close enough to touch. "You know it's true."

Kylo considered his father for a moment. "It's too late."

Han stepped yet closer. "No, it's not. Leave here with me. Come home. We miss you."

There was a long pause, and Kylo's face softened, his eyes shining with tears. "I'm being torn apart." His voice was strangled. "I want to be free of this pain. I know what I have to do, but I don't know if I have the strength to do it. Will you help me?"

Han stepped closer still. "Yes. Anything," he told his son.

Kylo dropped his helmet. He took out his lightsaber hilt, putting it into Han's hands. But at the last moment, just as the sky outside went dark, he ignited the red blade, driving it through his father.

Rey and Finn watched from a ledge high overhead as Han Solo touched his son's face one last time and toppled off the catwalk into the oscillator.

But Chewie was nearby, and he struck Kylo with his bowcaster, roaring in grief and rage at the loss of his friend. The Wookiee pressed the detonator, and fire exploded all over the vast cavern of the oscillator. Rey and Finn ran, and Kylo dragged himself to his feet and followed.

As for the oscillator, it had been damaged by the explosives but was still functional. The weapon would soon be able to fire.

Overhead, Poe turned his X-wing sideways, slipping into the narrow opening of the oscillator and bombing it with every weapon at his disposal, then slipping back out as the cavernous room exploded in a ball of flame. It wouldn't be long before the explosion worked its way through the entire base.

Rey and Finn hurried for the *Falcon*, but Rey heard the recognizable hum of Kylo Ren's lightsaber. He was waiting for them among the trees in the snow, just as she'd seen in her vision.

"It's just us now. Han Solo can't save you." Kylo grimaced as blood dripped from his side onto the snow.

Rey tried to attack, but Kylo used the Force to throw her against a tree. Finn ran to help her, and Kylo screamed, "Traitor!"

Hearing that word again, Finn stood and ignited Luke's blue lightsaber, which Maz had given to him on Takodana.

"That lightsaber," Kylo said. "It belongs to me."

"Come get it," Finn told him.

Their duel was quick and sharp, and Finn finally fell, unconscious. But when Kylo tried to call Luke's lightsaber to him using the Force, it flew right past him . . .

. . . and into Rey's hand!

The blue lightsaber felt right in Rey's grasp, but the planet's surface began to buckle and heave as groundquakes and fissures made every step perilous. Rey and Kylo dodged trees and rivers of lava as they dueled, his red saber against her blue one.

"You need a teacher," he told her, pressing her down with his blade. "I could show you the ways of the Force."

"The Force?"

Rey had forgotten—she had other powers at her disposal, powers she was just beginning to discover! She closed her eyes and focused, breathing calmly, and when she opened her eyes again, she had a new energy, a new focus.

The fight was like a dance for her then, whereas Kylo was struggling—and failing. She landed a major hit, and he fell to his knees. When he rose again, she slashed at his shoulder. Then she was the one stalking forward as he stumbled backward.

Finally, she slashed him across the face, and he fell to his back, wounded and panting. Just then, the ground bucked, and a new chasm opened between them. With one last look at her foe, Rey fled to help Finn.

But her friend was badly wounded and still unconscious. Rey bent over him crying. How would they ever escape the base before it exploded?

Suddenly, a bright light lit the forest around them: it was Chewie in the *Millennium Falcon*!

Together, Rey and Chewie got Finn on the ship and sped away from the unstable planet. Along with the remaining Resistance ships, they escaped to hyperspace just as Starkiller Base exploded!

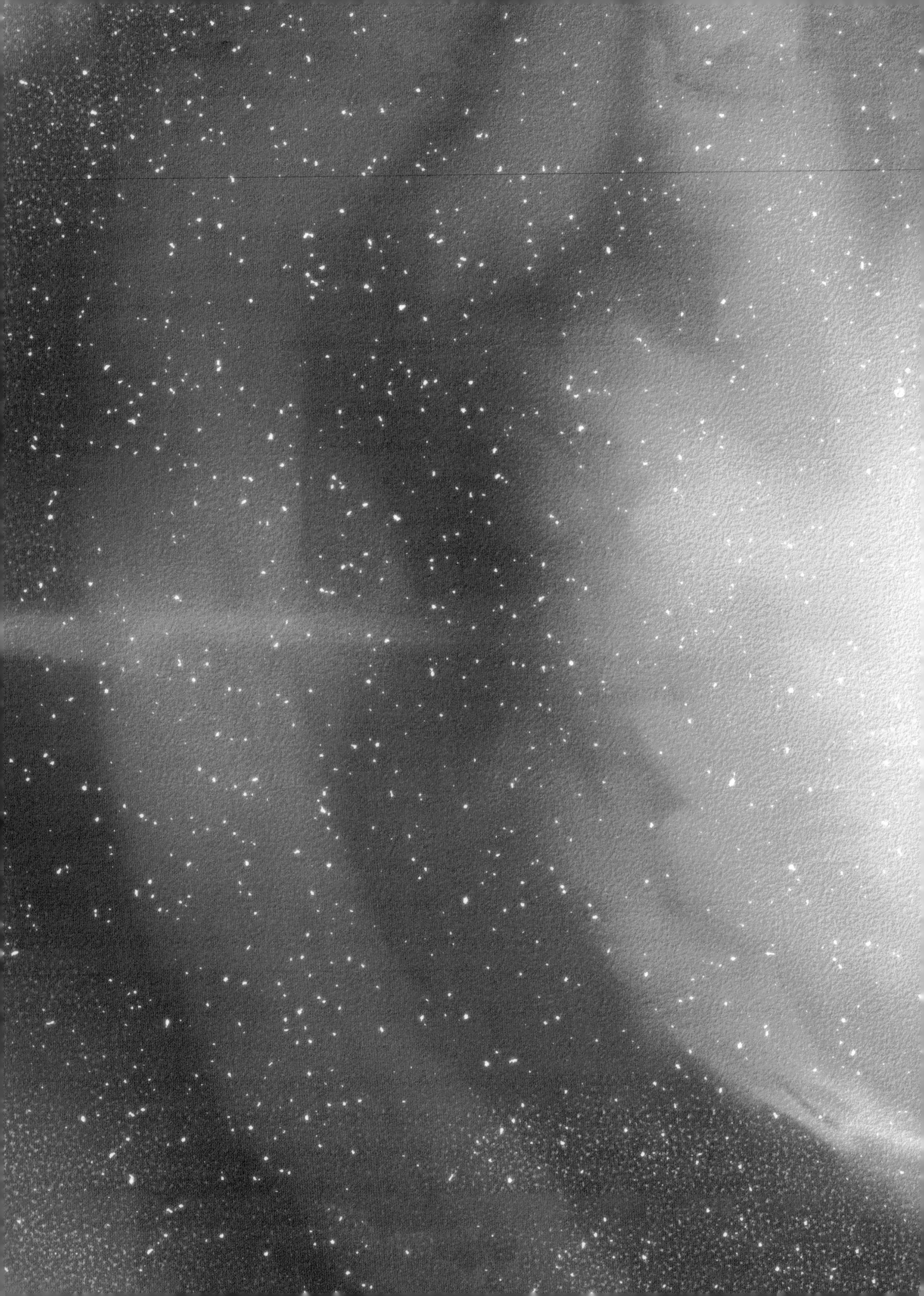

Back on D'Qar, Finn was taken to the medbay while Rey stood outside the *Falcon*, unsure what to say to General Organa. The older woman approached and drew Rey into a warm hug. Leia had felt Han leave the Force and was grieving him, too.

Deep in the Resistance base, however, BB-8 was excited: R2-D2 had finally woken up!

R2, BB-8, and C-3PO found Leia.

"Artoo may contain some much-needed good news," C-3PO told her.

R2 projected a star map, and when BB-8 likewise projected his part of the map, there it was: a path to Luke Skywalker!

Rey didn't want to leave without saying good-bye to Finn, but he was still unconscious.

"We'll see each other again," she promised, kissing his forehead gently.

Outside, General Organa took Rey's hands and told her, "May the Force be with you."

For all her loss, the older woman remained firm in her hope that things could still be set right.

Soon Rey sat in the *Millennium Falcon* beside Chewie as the Resistance gathered to cheer and wave them farewell.

The map's course was clear, and they shot into the sky.

When the *Falcon* emerged from hyperspace, Rey and Chewie looked down on a beautiful blue planet ringed in clouds. Landing on a rocky island she'd seen in her dreams, Rey walked up steep stairs, past calling shore birds, toward the settlement she could see high above.

Finally, she found what she sought.

A cloaked figure turned and pulled back his hood to reveal the face of Luke Skywalker!

Rey pulled Luke's lightsaber from her pack and held it out to the last Jedi.

He was her only hope.

THE LAST JEDI

The galaxy could not escape from war.

The Resistance had destroyed the First Order's superweapon, the Starkiller, but General Organa and her Resistance fighters were far from safe. With the New Republic defeated and the First Order fleet on its way to wipe out the Resistance base on the planet D'Qar, Leia's only hope was that she could evacuate her troops in time—and that Rey, the Force-sensitive scavenger, could find the last Jedi: Luke Skywalker.

The Resistance needed Luke to join the fight, to tip the scales against the dreaded First Order and return balance to the Force.

But Luke had hidden away for a reason, and Rey's mission would not be easy. . . .

On a remote island called Ahch-To, a young scavenger named Rey looked upon a legend, a hero, a savior—and the last Jedi.

Luke Skywalker.

She held out his lightsaber, the hopes of the galaxy reflected in her dark eyes. This man was the key to everything—saving the Resistance, ending tyranny, and yes, helping Rey understand her strange new connection with the mystical Force.

Luke took the lightsaber from Rey's hand and considered it carefully . . . then tossed it over his shoulder. With a grim expression, he set off down the stone steps Rey had just climbed to reach him. Rey followed him, confused. Did the long-lost Jedi Master not recognize his own weapon?

"Master Skywalker!" she called as he entered a crude village, went into a stone hut, and slammed the door. "I'm from the Resistance. Your sister, Leia, sent me. We need your help."

But there was no answer save the call of wild porgs, the fat feathered creatures that made their home on the island. Rey fetched the lightsaber from a grassy cliff and looked down at the water far below, where Luke's X-wing shimmered beneath turquoise waves.

In his hut, Luke considered the musty Jedi robes folded away in a trunk. There was another knock at his door.

"Go away!" he growled.

But the door burst inward, and a familiar figure barged inside: Luke's old friend Chewbacca!

"Chewie, what are you doing here?" Luke asked.

Chewie roared his response.

"He said you're coming back with us," Rey said.

Luke focused on her. "How did you find me?"

"Long story. We'll tell you on the *Falcon*."

"*Falcon*?" Luke asked. "Wait. Where's Han?"

But Chewie only looked down and moaned sadly.

High over D'Qar, First Order Star Destroyers and a Dreadnought appeared in the sky as the Resistance mounted an evacuation of its base. Their numbers were small, but they were determined to fight.

Leia watched in horror as her best pilot, Poe Dameron, and a squad of bombers, working against her orders, took out a key First Order ship . . . but lost much of the remaining Resistance fleet. With only seconds to spare, the Resistance

ships jumped to hyperspace and, they hoped, safety.

During the evacuation, Finn woke up in a bacta suit, healed from the beating he'd taken fighting Kylo Ren in the snowy forest of the First Order's destroyed Starkiller Base. The former First Order stormtrooper, now a Resistance hero, was lost and confused until he saw a familiar face.

"You must have a thousand questions," Poe said excitedly.

But Finn only had one. "Where's Rey?"

Aboard Supreme Leader Snoke's ship, the *Supremacy*, General Hux stood in a red-tinged throne room, surrounded by Snoke's Elite Praetorian Guard. Snoke sat on his throne in golden robes.

Snoke chuckled after Hux gave his report. "The Resistance will soon be in our grasp."

Hux thanked his leader and left as Kylo Ren entered and knelt.

"How's your wound?" Snoke asked Kylo, inquiring about the gash the scavenger Rey had given him during their battle on Starkiller Base.

"It's nothing," Kylo said from the ground, his voice flat through his mask.

Snoke stood before his apprentice. "When I found you, I saw what all masters live to see: raw, untamed power. And beyond that, something truly special: the potential of your bloodline. A new Vader." Snoke paused, considering. "Now I fear I was mistaken."

"I've given everything I have to you. To the dark side," Kylo argued.

Snoke gestured to Kylo's helmet. "Take that ridiculous thing off."

Kylo obeyed. His dark hair was messy, his face marred by the harsh slash of Rey's lightsaber.

"You have too much of your father's heart in you, young Solo."

"I *killed* Han Solo," Kylo hissed. "I didn't hesitate."

"And look at you. The deed split your spirit to the bone. You are unbalanced! Bested by a girl who had never held a lightsaber. You failed!" Snoke screamed.

Kylo rose, filled with fury, but Snoke threw him across the room using the Force. As he landed, Snoke's guards stepped forward, wielding their weapons to promise death to anyone who harmed their leader.

"Skywalker lives! The seed of the Jedi Order lives. As long as it does, hope lives in the galaxy. I thought you would be the one to snuff it out. Alas, you're no Vader." Snoke returned to his throne and sat heavily. "You're just a child in a mask."

On the way back to his quarters, Kylo considered his helmet—an homage to his grandfather Darth Vader, who had also worn a black helmet. Taking it in hand, he drove it into the walls, shattering glass and bending metal.

"Prepare my ship," he said to the first officers he saw.

Behind him, his helmet lay on the floor, broken and smoldering.

Cornered in his hut on Ahch-To by Chewie and the news of Han Solo's death, Luke Skywalker had little choice but to listen to Rey.

"There's no light left in Kylo Ren," she told him. "He's only getting stronger. The First Order will control all the major systems within weeks. We need your help. We need the Jedi Order back. We need Luke Skywalker."

Luke snorted. "You don't need Luke Skywalker. You think, what? I'm going to walk in with a laser sword and face down the whole First Order? Do you think I came to the most unfindable place in the galaxy for no reason at all?" He stood and left his hut. "Go away."

All day, Rey dogged Luke's steps, following him through the wind and rain. She watched him hike, fish, and milk a Thala-siren. Finally, as she chased him up a cliff, she heard something strange: voices calling to her. Looking down, she saw a jagged tree stump shrouded in fog. When she approached it, she discovered that it was hollow, and inside waited a cache of ancient tomes.

As Rey reached for a book, eyes alight with wonder, Luke appeared behind her. "Who are you?"

"I know this place," she told him.

"Built a thousand generations ago to keep these—the original Jedi texts." Luke took a book and opened it, showing the Jedi symbol of wings surrounding a shining light. "Just like me, they're the last of the Jedi religion." He turned to face her. "Why are you here?"

Rey considered it. "Something inside me has always been there. But now it's awake, and I'm afraid. I don't know what it is or what to do with it, and I need help."

"You need a teacher. But I can't teach you."

"Why not?" Rey hurried to face him. "I've seen your daily routine, and you're not busy."

"I will never train another generation of Jedi," Luke told her, his voice heavy with feeling. "I came to this island to die. It's time for the Jedi to end."

"Why? Leia sent me here with hope. If she was wrong, she deserves to know why."

But Luke just walked away.

Aboard the Resistance cruiser *Raddus*, Leia felt all her plans falling apart. She demoted Poe for his attack on the Dreadnought but was glad to see Finn, sharing with him that she had given Rey one of two beacons. Leia held the other. The beacon would help Rey find the Resistance again, once she'd discovered Luke. Now the Resistance needed to find a new base that was strong enough to send a signal to its allies, requesting help.

But soon an impossible thing happened: even though no one had ever been able to track ships through hyperspace, the First Order had found them! With only enough fuel left for one more jump to lightspeed, the Resistance ships had to get out of range of the First Order.

Poe and his pilots ran to their ships, but Kylo Ren led the First Order TIE fighters, and his first run destroyed the Resistance hangar. Poe's ship, like so many others, was consumed by fire.

From his TIE silencer, Kylo next focused on the command room, his finger on the trigger that would certainly kill his own mother.

But he stopped at the last moment—he could feel her in the Force. It didn't matter, though—the rest of his squadron fired, and General Organa was sucked out into space.

Leia floated free, frost forming on her skin. Death was mere seconds away when her eyes opened and she did something she'd never done before: she used the Force to pull herself back into the ship!

Long before, Yoda had told Luke that the Force ran strong in his family. Leia had reached deep within and accessed that power.

As she was taken to the medbay, Leia dropped the beacon she had carried for Rey. Finn picked it up. The Resistance faced many obstacles, but his most important task was keeping Rey safe.

It was nighttime on Ahch-To, and Luke slipped into the *Millennium Falcon* by himself, haunted by memories. Across the ship, R2-D2 woke up and beeped excitedly, telling his master everything.

"Old friend," Luke said, patting him. "I wish I could make you understand, but I'm not coming back. Nothing could make me change my mind."

R2 considered that, and then he replayed a very old hologram of a beautiful girl in white robes. It was the original holo that had begun Luke's entire adventure and led him to his sister, his friends, his Jedi studies, and even his own father's redemption.

"This is our most desperate hour," young Leia pled. "Help me, Obi-Wan Kenobi. You're my only hope."

Luke sighed heavily. He knew what he had to do.

Rey woke with a gasp to find Luke standing over her.

"Tomorrow, at dawn," he said. "Three lessons. I will teach you the ways of the Jedi. And why they need to end."

With Leia unconscious but recovering and most of the other leadership lost in the explosion, Vice Admiral Holdo was announced as the new leader of the Resistance. Poe couldn't help thinking that Holdo, a willowy older woman with lilac hair and a mauve dress, was an odd choice; nevertheless, she stood before what was left of the Resistance.

"Four hundred of us on three ships. We're the very last of the Resistance, but we're not alone. In every corner of the galaxy, the downtrodden and oppressed know our symbol and they put their hope in it. We are the spark that will light the fire that will restore the Republic. That spark, this Resistance, must survive. That is our mission. Now, to your stations, and may the Force be with us."

But when Poe attempted to speak with Holdo, she did not want to hear his plans.

"I've dealt with plenty of trigger-happy flyboys like you. You're impulsive, dangerous, and the last thing we need right now. So stick to your post, and follow my orders," she told him.

Finn had packed a bag to leave and find Rey, but he was stopped by a Resistance mechanic named Rose. She had heard Finn was a hero, but when she realized he was trying to steal an escape pod, she was disappointed to learn that he was just another coward. Rose was still distraught from the death of her sister, Paige, who had been in one of the Resistance bombers during the earlier battle, but she knew what she had to do. Rose stunned Finn and began dragging him to the brig to report him for desertion.

"My sister died protecting the fleet, and you were just running away," she told Finn as he woke up.

"This fleet is doomed," Finn said, still unable to move.

Rose was disgusted. "You're a selfish traitor."

But Finn had to convince her. "We can't outrun the First Order. They can track us through lightspeed! If we jump, they show up thirty seconds later, and we'd have used a ton of fuel, which we're dangerously short on."

Rose was a genius with machines, and she immediately understood how the First Order's tracking worked. "Active tracking. It's new tech, but the principle must be the same as any active tracker, so they're only tracking us . . ."

"From the lead ship," Finn finished with her. They realized that with Rose's tech expertise and Finn's knowledge of First Order ships, they could work together to shut down the tracker so the Resistance could escape.

When they explained their idea to Poe, he decided he would help them . . . without telling Vice Admiral Holdo. If she didn't trust him with her plans, there was no need to share his own. Finn and Rose just needed a way past the First Order's clearance codes. Poe called their old friend Maz Kanata, who recommended a master codebreaker. Rose and Finn would find him wearing a red plom bloom at the high-stakes table of a casino in Canto Bight.

Before he and Rose left on their mission, Finn gave Rey's tracking beacon to Poe, the only person he trusted to keep it safe.

As Rey awoke in her hut on Ahch-To, she felt something strange, a new ripple in the Force. She heard a man breathing, and she knew somehow that it was Kylo Ren. Sure enough, when she sat up in bed, he stood before her. She swiftly shot him with her blaster, but . . . he was no longer there. She went outside and found no one . . . but then, suddenly, Kylo Ren appeared again. He was there, and yet he was not physically present. Without his black cloak and helmet, he seemed different somehow, but his reaction was just as she'd expected: he held out a gloved hand and said, "You'll bring Luke Skywalker to me."

When that didn't work, he sat back and sighed. "You're not doing this. The effort would kill you." He looked around. "Can you see my surroundings?"

"You're gonna pay for what you did!" Rey growled, ignoring his question.

But he went on as if she hadn't spoken. "I can't see yours. Just you. So, no. This is something else."

Behind Rey, Luke emerged from his hut and pointed at the hole she'd shot in her own hut's stone wall. "What's that about?"

The village's fishlike alien Caretakers were annoyed with Rey, but Rey was too worried that Kylo could see where she was, could sense that she was with Luke. When she turned back around, Kylo Ren had disappeared.

"I was cleaning my blaster and it went off." Rey fumbled over the excuse. She didn't like lying to Luke, but she didn't know what had just happened, and she didn't want to risk the chance that the Jedi Master wouldn't teach her.

"Let's get started," he said.

Luke led Rey up a set of ancient stairs through a stone cavern, the path worn by innumerable footsteps. They passed a mosaic of the Jedi symbol, and Luke stopped at a stone altar that stood high over the ocean below.

"What do you know about the Force?" he asked.

"It's a power that Jedi have that lets them control people and . . . make things float," she answered.

Luke shook his head. "Impressive. Every word in that sentence was wrong. Now, first lesson. Sit here, legs crossed."

Rey got up on the rock and sat.

"The Force is not a power you have," Luke continued. "It's not about lifting rocks. It's the energy between all things. The tension, the balance that binds the universe together. Close your eyes. Breathe. Now, reach out."

Rey reached out her hand.

"I feel something!" she gasped.

"That's the Force! Wow, it must be really strong with you!"

"I've never felt any — *ow!*"

Something had smacked her hand, and when she opened her eyes in surprise, she found Luke holding the heavy blade of grass he'd used to tickle and then slap her outstretched fingers.

"You meant reach out like . . ." Rey's voice trailed off as she realized that he had intended for her to reach out with her mind.

Luke's wry look confirmed it. He put her hand on the rock.

"Reach out with your feelings. What do you see?"

Rey began to feel it. "The island. Life. Death and decay that feeds new life. Warmth. Cold. Peace. Violence."

"And between it all?" Luke urged.

"Balance and energy." Rey smiled. "A force."

"And inside you?"

"Inside me — that same force."

"And this is the lesson: that force does not belong to the Jedi. To say that if the Jedi die the light dies is vanity. Can you feel that?"

"Yes, but . . . there's something else. Beneath the island. A dark place." She could see it in her mind, a deep hole surrounded by vines.

"Balance," Luke reminded her. "Powerful light, powerful darkness."

Around Rey, the mountain began to split. "It's calling me," she said.

"Resist it, Rey!" Luke shouted.

But she couldn't see him, couldn't hear him. Her mind plummeted into that cold, dark hole until seawater erupted upward, soaking her.

"You went straight to the dark," Luke told her, horrified.

"That place was trying to show me something," she countered.

"It offered you something you needed, and you didn't even try to stop yourself."

But Rey had noticed something else. "I didn't see you," she told Luke. "You've closed yourself off from the Force."

Luke gave her a guilty look. "I've seen this raw strength only once before — in Ben Solo. It didn't scare me enough then. It does now."

Luke turned away, disappointed — and frightened.

"Lesson two," Luke told Rey the next day. "Now that they're extinct, the Jedi are romanticized, as if they were gods. But when you strip away the myth and look at their deeds, the legacy of the Jedi is failure."

He was leading Rey back to the ancient temple.

"At the height of their powers, they allowed Darth Sidious to rise, create the Empire, and wipe them out. It was a Jedi Master who was responsible for the training and creation of Darth Vader."

"And a Jedi who saved him," Rey countered. "You saw the conflict inside him. You believed he could be turned!"

"And I became a legend," Luke reluctantly agreed. "For many years, there was balance, and then I saw . . . Ben. My nephew. With that mighty Skywalker blood. With my hubris, I thought I could train him, pass on my strengths. Leia trusted me with her son. I took him and a dozen students and began a training temple."

Luke began to pace the stone room.

"By the time I realized I was no match for the darkness rising in him, it was too late. I went to confront him, and he turned on me. He must've thought I was dead. When I came to, the temple was burning. He had vanished with a handful of my students and slaughtered the rest. Leia blamed Snoke, but it was me. I failed. Because I was Luke Skywalker. Jedi Master." Luke turned to face Rey. "A legend."

"The galaxy may need a legend," she said. "I need someone to show me my place in all this. And you didn't fail Kylo. Kylo failed you." She gave him a defiant look. "I won't."

Meanwhile, across the galaxy, Finn and Rose had landed in Canto Bight on the planet Cantonica. As they wandered into a posh casino, Finn was struck by the beauty that surrounded him. Everything glittered. Wealthy patrons passed by, draped in the finest clothes and jewels, sipping luxurious beverages. The shining room shook as fathiers, powerful horselike creatures, thundered around a track nearby. The place radiated with glamour.

"This place is great!" Finn exclaimed.

But Rose looked disgusted.

"Who do you think these people are?" Rose asked him. "There's only one business in the galaxy that will get you this rich – selling weapons to the First Order. I wish I could put my fist through this whole lousy beautiful town."

Finn looked around and saw the place with fresh eyes, just as BB-8 rolled up beeping about a red plom bloom. The Master Codebreaker they were looking for was playing at a high-stakes table nearby.

But before they could approach him, they were apprehended by local police!

Rose and Finn were thrown in jail for illegally parking their shuttle on one of Canto Bight's beaches. The two friends discussed their options. What were they going to do? How were they going to get out? And even if they *could* get out, how would they find another codebreaker to get past the First Order's clearance codes so they could deactivate the tracker? Rose and Finn were close to giving up hope. They knew that the Resistance fleet didn't have any time to spare — they were running out of fuel and could only outrun the First Order for so long.

Suddenly, their cell mate, an unkempt man called DJ, roused to life in the corner. They had thought he was passed out, but he was listening to their conversation.

"Codebreaker? Thief?" DJ asked. "I can do it. Me and the First Order codeage go way back."

"We're — we got it covered," Rose replied, unsure about going into business with such a character.

DJ shrugged, got up, and with some quick handiwork, opened their cell door and walked right out.

Rose and Finn were baffled, but they took their chance to escape, slipping under a sewer grate as they heard police running through the halls after them.

Rose and Finn emerged in the fathier stables.

Three young stable hands almost turned them in to the authorities, but Rose showed them her ring, which had a hidden Resistance crest. With the children's help, Rose and Finn escaped the guards by crashing through the casino and down city streets on the back of one of the powerful creatures. But their fathier soon skidded to a halt at the edge of a cliff. They had reached a dead end. The authorities would trap them soon enough.

Rose removed the fathier's saddle and urged the beast to run away, to finally be free.

Just as the police closed in, a sleek ship rose in front of them — it was DJ and BB-8! Finn and Rose climbed on board, and they rocketed off into space. They could continue their mission. They had a codebreaker, whether he was the one they wanted or not.

Rey was walking on Ahch-To one night when she felt the connection with Kylo Ren again.

"I'd rather not do this now," she informed him.

"Yeah, me too," he replied.

"Why did you hate your father?" she asked, tears threatening. "You had a father who loved you!"

Kylo stepped forward. "I didn't hate him."

"Then why did you kill him?"

"Your parents threw you away like garbage, but you can't stop needing them. It's your greatest weakness. Looking for them everywhere—in Han Solo, now in Skywalker." Kylo paused. "Did he tell you what happened that night?"

"Yes!"

"No. He had sensed my power, as he senses yours, and he feared it." Kylo showed her a vision of himself, younger, waking up to find Luke standing over him with his lightsaber drawn. In the vision, young Kylo lit his own lightsaber to block the killing stroke, then used the Force to pull the temple down on top of his master.

"Liar," Rey spat.

But Kylo remained calm and strangely pitying.

"Let the past die," he said. "Kill it, if you have to. That's the only way to become what you were meant to be."

Rey turned away, tears in her eyes.

She had called Kylo a liar, and yet she sensed that he was telling the truth. She didn't know how to feel about Luke anymore.

As she stood there, trying to understand what was happening, she felt it again: the call toward the hole in the cliffs, the cold place Luke had warned her to resist. Her feet led her there, and she held out a hand to it and fell in, landing in an underground pool.

When Rey crawled out of the water, she found a dark mirror holding many copies of her image.

No matter which way she looked, she saw only endless versions of herself.

"I should've felt trapped or panicked," she later told Kylo through another Force vision as she sat in her hut. "But I didn't. It was leading somewhere, and at the end, it would show me what I'd come to see."

Rey had begged the vision to reveal her parents, and two dark shadows had approached the mirror and merged into one figure, which matched its hand to hers. But when the frost over the glass cleared, she saw only . . . herself.

"I thought I'd find answers here," she said, forlorn. "I was wrong. I'd never felt so alone."

"You're not alone," Kylo whispered.

"Neither are you," she told him. "It isn't too late."

She held out a hand, and he removed his glove and reached for her. Their fingers touched, and a tear slipped down Rey's cheek.

Just then, Luke burst through the door of her hut, saw the Force vision of Kylo, and yelled, "Stop!"

The hut exploded around them, and Rey stood, furious.

"Is it true? Did you try to murder him?" she shouted through the rain.

"Leave this island now!" Luke shouted back.

He spun and marched away.

But Rey was done with Luke's avoidance. She wanted the truth, so she followed him, ordering him to stop.

When he didn't, she hit him in the back with her staff, knocking him to the ground. "Did you create Kylo Ren?"

Luke stood and grabbed a staff of his own to block her attacks. When he knocked her staff out of her hands, Rey used the Force to grasp and ignite her blue lightsaber, which had once been Luke's.

But she didn't try to strike him down. She deactivated the blade and said, "Tell me the truth."

"I saw darkness," Luke confessed. "I'd sensed it building in him. I'd seen it in moments of his training. But then I looked inside, and it was beyond what I'd ever imagined. Snoke had already turned his heart. He would bring destruction and pain and death and the end of everything I love because of what he would become, and for the briefest moment of pure instinct, I thought I could stop it. But it passed like a fleeting shadow, and I was left with shame. The last thing I saw were the eyes of a frightened boy whose master had failed him."

"You failed him by thinking his choice was made. It wasn't," Rey argued. "There's still conflict in him. If he would turn from the dark side, that would shift the tide. This could be how we win."

"This is not going to go the way you think!" Luke barked.

But Rey was confident. "It is. Just now, when we touched hands, I saw his future, as solid as I see you. If I go to him, Ben Solo will turn."

"Rey, don't do this."

Rey stood and held out Luke's lightsaber, just as she had on first meeting him.

Still he didn't take it.

"Then he's our last hope," she said sadly. She turned, picked up her staff, and left.

Luke watched the *Millennium Falcon* blast away.

After putting on his old Jedi robes, he walked to the ancient tree that held the sacred texts, carrying a burning torch. But he wasn't alone as he'd thought. An old friend had followed him.

"Master Yoda," Luke said, turning to stare at the Force ghost of his old master.

"Young Skywalker," Yoda greeted him.

"I'm ending all this. The tree, the texts, the Jedi. I'm going to burn it down," Luke told him. But Luke paused, his torch centimeters from the tree.

"Hmmm." Yoda closed his eyes, and lightning struck the tree, which burst into flame. Yoda laughed and laughed. "Ah, Skywalker. Missed you, have I."

Luke ran to the tree, regretting what he'd planned to do, but he was thrown back by an explosion. He had no choice but to watch the Jedi tree burn.

"So it is time for the Jedi Order to end," Luke said with great finality.

"Time it is" — Yoda hobbled toward him — "for you to look past a pile of old books, hmmm?"

"They're sacred Jedi texts!" Luke shouted.

"Oh!" Yoda cocked his head. "Read them, have you? Page turners, they were not. Wisdom they held, but that library contained nothing that the girl Rey does not already possess. Hmmm. Skywalker. Still looking to the horizon." Yoda hobbled closer. "Never here, now, hmmm? The need in front of your nose."

The Force ghost bopped Luke in the face with his spectral cane.

"I was weak . . . unwise . . ." Luke began.

"Lost Ben Solo, you did. Lose Rey, we must not."

"I can't be what she needs me to be," Luke growled.

"Heeded my words not, did you. Pass on what you have learned. Strength, mastery. But weakness, folly, failure also. Yes! Failure most of all. The greatest teacher, failure is."

Yoda sat beside Luke, and they watched the tree burn.

"Luke, we are what they grow beyond. That is the true burden of all masters."

Rey knew what she had to do.

On board the *Falcon*, she climbed into one of the ship's escape pods and set a course for the *Supremacy.* Then Chewie and the *Falcon* disappeared into hyperspace. When her pod landed in the First Order hangar, Kylo Ren was there – but he had Rey put in binders before he led her away.

"You don't have to do this," she told him. "I feel the conflict in you. It's tearing you apart. Ben, when we touched hands, I saw your future. You will not bow before Snoke. You'll turn. I'll help you. I saw it."

"I saw something, too," he said. "I know that when the moment comes, *you'll* be the one to turn. You'll stand with me. Rey, I saw who your parents are."

When the next door opened, Rey saw Snoke sitting on his throne, flanked by his red-clad guards. Kylo escorted her forward.

"Well done, my apprentice," Snoke said, cackling. "My faith in you is restored."

He turned to Rey.

"Young Rey. Welcome. Come closer, child. So much strength. Darkness rises, and light to meet it. I warned my young apprentice that as he grew stronger, his equal in the light would rise."

Snoke held out a hand, and Luke's lightsaber flew from Kylo's hand to his own. "Skywalker, I'd assumed." Snoke chuckled. "Wrongly. Come closer, I said."

When Rey didn't move, he used the Force to pull her near.

"You underestimate Skywalker. And Ben Solo. And me," Rey told him with certainty. "It will be your downfall."

"Have you seen a weakness in my apprentice?" Snoke asked, laughing at her. "Young fool. It was I who bridged your minds. I stoked Ren's conflicted soul. I knew he was not strong enough to hide it from you. And you were not wise enough to resist the bait. And now, you will give me Skywalker, and then I will kill you with the cruelest stroke."

Snoke forced his way into Rey's mind. As she screamed in pain, Kylo's resolve began to weaken.

Rey tried to use the Force to snatch her lightsaber, but Snoke merely smacked her in the head with it before placing it next to him. Rey used the Force to steal Kylo's red lightsaber, but Snoke's guards surrounded her, weapons at the ready.

"And still that fiery spit of hope," Snoke heckled. "You have the spirit of a true Jedi."

When she attacked him, he again used his superior Force powers to toss her away.

"And because of that, you must die."

He spun Rey around to face Kylo.

"My worthy apprentice, heir apparent to Lord Vader, where there was conflict, I now sense resolve. Where there was weakness, strength. Complete your training and fulfill your destiny!"

Kylo picked up his saber and faced Rey. "I know what I have to do."

"Ben!" she cried in anguish.

Snoke laughed. "You think you can turn him? I cannot be betrayed or beaten. I see his mind. I see his every intent. Yes. I see him turning the lightsaber to strike true."

At Snoke's side, silently, Rey's lightsaber did indeed turn.

"And now, foolish child, he ignites it and kills his true enemy!"

But instead of igniting the red lightsaber in his hand, Kylo used the Force to ignite Luke's saber, slicing his master in half!

Supreme Leader Snoke was dead.

The blue lightsaber flew to Rey's hand, and she and Kylo faced each other, both lightsabers at the ready. They turned back to back to battle Snoke's guards, taking them down one by one, fighting as if they'd trained together for years. Finally, the throne room was still. They were alone.

"Order them to stop firing," Rey said, pointing at the First Order ships chasing the Resistance fleet out in space. "There's still time to save the fleet."

But Kylo only said, "It's time to let old things die. Snoke. Skywalker. The Sith. The Jedi. The rebels. Let it all die."

He held out his hand.

"Join me. We can rule together and bring a new order to the galaxy."

"Don't do this, Ben," Rey begged.

"No! You're still holding on!" He withdrew his hand. "Do you still want to know the truth about your parents? Have you always known, or have you hidden it away?" He stepped toward her. "You know the truth. Say it."

"They were nobody." Tears streaked down Rey's face.

"They were filthy junk traders," Kylo agreed. "Who sold you off for drinking money. You have no place in this story. You're nothing." He met her eyes. "But not to me. Join me."

Again, he held out his hand. "Please."

Little did Rey know that her friends were also on board the *Supremacy*. DJ had gotten Rose, Finn, and BB-8 through the difficult clearance codes and onto the ship, where they had dressed in First Order uniforms to avoid detection.

But when DJ opened the door to the tracking system, they found something unexpected: a welcoming party of First Order officers and troopers, led by Captain Phasma!

DJ had betrayed them.

As they were forced to kneel before Captain Phasma, Rose and Finn learned that DJ had earned his freedom by striking a deal: he had told the First Order about the Resistance's plan to secretly evacuate their transports and land on the nearby planet Crait. He had overheard Poe telling Finn the plan through his comlink

during their journey from Canto Bight to the *Supremacy*, and now the First Order knew exactly where to strike.

General Hux gave the order to fire on the Resistance transports, and Rose and Finn watched as the defenseless ships were destroyed one by one. Not only had their plan failed, but because of them, their friends were in terrible danger.

Back in Snoke's throne room, Rey knew she was in danger, too. She reached out as if to take Kylo's hand, but instead she used the Force to grab her lightsaber — or try to.

The saber froze in the air as Kylo bent his own Force powers to the task. They were evenly matched, and the weapon floated between them as they fought for control.

On the Resistance's main cruiser, the *Raddus*, Vice Admiral Holdo had stayed behind to pilot the ship so Leia and the rest of the Resistance troops would have a better chance of escaping to the surface of Crait.

Before convincing Poe to depart, she'd reminded him of one of Leia's favorite quotes: "Hope is like the sun. If you only believe it when you can see it, you'll never make it through the night."

With great calm and fierce will, Vice Admiral Holdo aimed the *Raddus* at the *Supremacy* and jumped to lightspeed, cutting the First Order's flagship in half and crippling its fleet.

At the same time, the lightsaber hovering between Rey and Kylo Ren exploded in a shower of sparks.

The *Supremacy* rocked with explosions. All was chaos. Captain Phasma had been on the verge of executing Rose and Finn, but now the hangar was on fire. Phasma and her troopers took aim at their prisoners, but an AT-ST walker fought loose from its moorings and started blasting the chrome-plated trooper. It was piloted by BB-8! Phasma, however, wasn't done. She attacked Finn with a spear, and he fought back with a laser axe. Phasma knocked Finn through a hole in the floor, but he rose

up and slashed her viciously with his axe. Her helmet shattered, showing a sliver of her face for the first time, her icy-blue eye filled with fury.

"You were always scum," she said.

"Rebel scum," Finn replied.

Before Phasma could respond, the floor underneath her gave way, and she plummeted into a fiery abyss. Rose, Finn, and BB-8 managed to escape the destruction in a stolen First Order shuttle, and set off to rejoin the Resistance on Crait.

Across the ship, General Hux found Kylo in Snoke's destroyed throne room.

"What happened?"

Rey had managed to grab the broken pieces of Luke's lightsaber and hop in Snoke's escape craft before Kylo regained consciousness.

"The girl murdered Snoke," Kylo lied. "Let's finish this."

"Finish this?" Hux growled. "You presume to command my army? We have no ruler — "

But Kylo Ren used the Force to choke General Hux, revealing who was really in charge.

"The Supreme Leader is dead," Kylo began.

"Long live the Supreme Leader," Hux finished.

Kylo Ren would lead the First Order.

On the salt-crusted planet Crait, Rose and Finn barely skidded into the old rebel base where the Resistance had gathered before the heavy blast door closed. After emerging from her coma, Leia had ordered the Resistance to send out a distress signal to the Outer Rim.

"If there are any allies to the Resistance, it's now or never," Leia said.

"Let's just pray that big door holds long enough to get us some help," Poe added.

But Finn saw a First Order siege cannon approaching, and there was no other way out of

the base, which was one big cave. The Resistance had to buy time for their allies to arrive, and their only chance was to take out the cannon using ancient ski speeders that had been rusting in the base since the days of the Rebel Alliance. As the rattling relics skimmed over the ground, they kicked up red plumes of clay that lay under the salt.

The ski speeders were taking major hits from the First Order's TIE fighters, AT-M6 walkers, and AT-ATs until a miracle happened: the *Millennium Falcon* showed up!

Rey took out TIEs from the gunner seat while Chewie roared at the controls. By his side, a porg flapped its wings and shrieked a battle cry of its own.

"Oh, they *hate* that ship!" Finn shouted as their enemies trailed off to follow the infamous Corellian freighter.

Seeing an opening, Finn aimed his speeder right for the center of the charged cannon, ready to sacrifice himself to save what was left of the Resistance.

"Retreat, Finn! That's an order!" Poe called.

"No! I won't let them win!" Finn replied.

But at the last minute, Rose plowed her speeder into Finn's from the side, causing him to skid off course. Finn climbed from the wreckage and went to where Rose lay, wounded amid the debris of her own speeder.

"Why did you stop me?" he demanded.

She smiled.

"I saved you, dummy. That's how we're going to win. Not fighting what we hate. Saving what we love."

As the siege cannon blew open the armored door of the Resistance base, she lifted her face to kiss Finn . . . and then fell unconscious.

Inside the base, the Resistance learned that although the distress signal had been heard, no one was coming to help them.

"We fought to the end," Leia said sadly. "But the galaxy has lost all its hope. The spark . . . is out."

But then she looked up, surprised. A hooded figure approached her through the gloom.

"Luke!" she said as he sat down to face her. "I know what you're going to say. I changed my hair."

"It's nice that way," he told her. "Leia . . . I'm sorry."

"I know. I know you are. I'm just glad you're here, at the end."

"I came to face him, Leia. And I can't save him."

"I held out hope for so long, but . . ." Leia shook her head. "I know my son's gone."

"No one's ever really gone," Luke assured her.

Leia reached out, and they held hands. Luke kissed her on the forehead and walked through the gaping hole in the door.

As Luke stood there in his black robes, every First Order gun aimed at him—and fired. A great column of red soil exploded from where he'd been standing, but an odd thing happened: Luke walked right out of the smoke, unharmed!

He brushed a bit of debris off his shoulder and waited.

"We have to help him," Finn said as he looked out at Luke standing by himself on the battlefield. "We have to fight!"

But Poe shook his head. He finally understood that running out to fight wasn't always the answer.

"We are the spark that will light the fire that'll burn the First Order down. Skywalker's doing this so we can survive."

Although the droids couldn't find a way out of the old base, the Resistance followed the chiming of strange crystal foxes that lived inside the cave, hoping the creatures would lead them outside. But when they reached the end of the tunnel, they found only heavy boulders and a hole so narrow that no person could squeeze through.

Little did they know that on the other side of the rock wall, Rey was waiting for them. She had used the beacon that Leia had given her to track

down her friends. Rey watched the last crystal fox wiggle through the small opening in the boulders. She knew what she had to do.

"Lifting rocks," Rey said to herself, shaking her head in amusement.

On the battlefield, Kylo Ren's shuttle had landed in front of the Jedi Master. Luke's former student strode out to meet him.

"Did you come back to save me?" Kylo asked.

"No," Luke answered.

Kylo slipped off his outer robes and lit his red lightsaber, and Luke lit his blue one, the Jedi Master ready to duel his nephew and former apprentice. Kylo was furious and powerful, but Luke remained ever tranquil. Again and again, Kylo attacked him. Again and again, Luke calmly, casually repelled him.

"I failed you, Ben. I'm sorry," Luke said.

"I'm sure you are," Kylo spat back. "The Resistance is dead. The war is over. And when I kill you, I will have killed the last Jedi!"

Luke shook his head. "Amazing. Every word of what you just said was wrong. The rebellion is reborn today. The war is just beginning. And I will not be the last Jedi."

"I'll destroy her. And you. And all of it," Kylo promised.

For just a moment, Luke paused. Kylo Ren hadn't sensed it, but Luke knew that Rey had used the Force to lift all the rocks blocking the exit so the Resistance could escape from the cave.

"No," Luke replied. "Strike me down in anger, and I'll always be with you. Just like your father."

Kylo ran for him and swung his red saber through Luke's chest—but nothing happened. Luke still stood, unharmed. He slowly turned to face Kylo Ren, but no matter how many times Kylo struck him, Luke did not fall.

"See you around, kid," Luke said.

And with that, Luke Skywalker disappeared before Kylo's eyes.

Far away on Ahch-To, Luke fell to the ground. He had been meditating, using the Force to appear on Crait.

His sacrifice had saved his sister, his new apprentice, and everyone he loved. He had helped the Resistance survive to keep fighting the First Order.

As Luke stared off into the setting twin suns of the ancient Jedi island, so like the twin suns he'd once watched set on Tatooine, his robes fluttered to the stone. He'd witnessed Obi-Wan and Yoda become one with the Force, and now it was Luke's turn to join them.

Rey helped the last Resistance member on board the *Falcon* and turned. She felt her connection with Kylo Ren again, felt him still calling to her. But she didn't heed it. She closed the *Falcon*'s ramp — and closed herself off to Kylo Ren.

But for Rey, new doors were opening. She met Poe, was reunited with Finn and Leia, fixed BB-8's antenna, and ran a hand over the ancient Jedi texts she'd smuggled away from the old tree on Ahch-To before she left.

"Luke is gone?" she asked Leia. "I felt it. But it wasn't sadness or pain. It was peace and purpose."

"I felt it, too," Leia assured her.

"How do we build the rebellion from this?" Rey asked, looking around at the few others on board, all that remained of the Resistance. She held in her hands the pieces of Luke's broken lightsaber.

Leia clasped Rey's hand and gave her a knowing smile.

"We have everything we need."

Leia was right.

The Resistance had hope, and with hope — as the past had shown them — they could do anything.

The story concludes in . . .

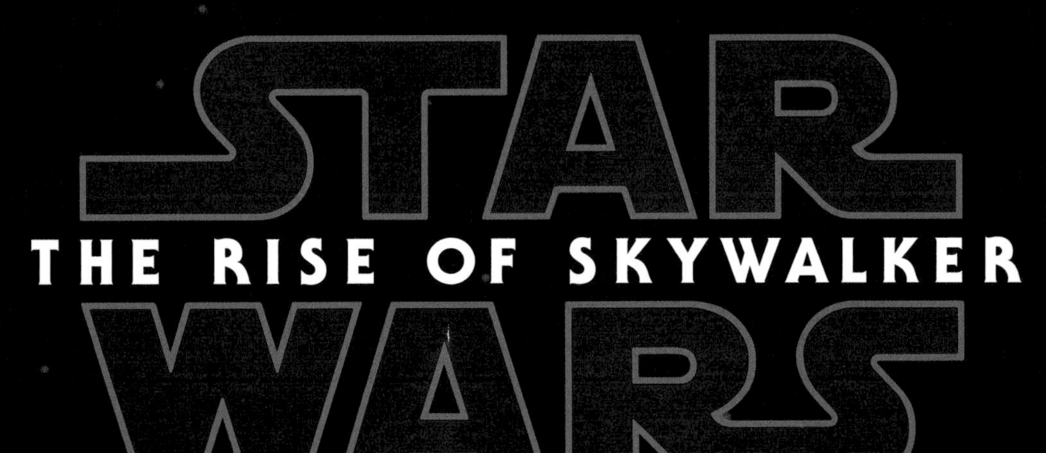

DELILAH S. DAWSON

Delilah S. Dawson is the *New York Times* best-selling author of *Star Wars: Phasma*, as well as *Star Wars: Black Spire*, *Star Wars: The Perfect Weapon*, the Shadow series (as Lila Bowen), the Hit series, the Tales of Pell (with Kevin Hearne), and a variety of short stories and comics. She lives in Florida with her family.

BRIAN ROOD

Brian Rood is a professional illustrator working throughout the entertainment industry, but he has spent the better part of a decade working primarily in a galaxy far, far away. When he's not busy in his studio creating new artwork for the *Star Wars* universe, he is spending time with his wife and two children in southern Michigan.